The Royal Diaries

ANACAONA

GOLDEN FLOWER

BY EDWIDGE DANTICAT

Scholastic Inc. New York

HAITI
1490

AUTHOR'S NOTE

Unlike most other young women of the Royal Diary series, Anacaona did not read or write and would not have kept a diary in the traditional sense of written accounts of her daily life. Anacaona's Taíno people, however, had many other ways of recording things crucial to them. They passed on their stories, myths, cultural practices, and ways of healing through songs, dances, and ballads that were performed at their feasts and celebrations, called areitos. *Even though the Taínos had no written language, they had petroglyphs — rock paintings and pictographs through which they kept records of their lives. Additionally, the Taínos measured time through agricultural seasons and a lunar calendar, and did not count beyond twenty — their number of fingers and toes. To present the story of this brilliant Taíno woman leader in her early adulthood, we have imagined her thoughts and experiences and how she might have kept track of them using a twenty-day lunar cycle. We hope some sense of her own wisdom and that of her people is conveyed in this fictional story of the real Anacaona.*

I am Anacaona.

In my language, the Taíno language, *ana* means "flower" and *caona* means "golden." Thus I am called the "golden flower." I have received a great gift from Cuybio, the weaver of my uncle, who is the *cacique*, or supreme chief, of Xaraguá. (Out of respect, we call my uncle Matunherí, which means "Most Highest One.") Cuybio has found a way to blend cotton buds into a hard fabric on which I can record my stories, ballads, and some other knowledge that is important to our people. He has seen me many times carving symbols on the plaza walls outside the temple and has remarked that he must find yet another manner for Matunherí's niece, one of Xaraguá's possible future rulers, to record these symbols.

My older brother, Behechio, has already reminded me many times that this is a very important offering Cuybio has made to me and I must resist the temptation to use Cuybio's creation in its entirety by sunset.

As is our custom, my mother and I began our day with a bath in the river. Before sunrise, the river is clear and tranquil, and as we put our feet in, both Bibi and I were able to see our reflections floating on the surface, then slowly widening and moving away from us in a ripple of expanding rings. Just then I had a vision that we were receiving a message from the *opia*, the spirits of our vanished ancestors, preparing us for something to come.

I have been having these visions since my head came up only as high as Bibi's knees. Now our heads almost touch when we stand close to one another in the river, scrubbing our skins with cleansing *digo* plants.

In between the pebbles in the riverbed lie chunks of golden stones, which have been carried down from the mountains with the river flow. When the sun shines on these shales, they glow in such a way that they seem to be trying to prove their own brilliance to the sky. Before our bath, Bibi and I stopped to collect a few. Later, we flattened them, looped them on cotton ropes, and wore them around our arms and legs. Soon I will come to a season in my life when I will be a *siani*, a married woman, like my mother.

There have been several births in the villages, the most notable being the child of Cuybio's younger sister, Yeybona. Yeybona was born only a few moons before me. I heard many of those who gathered in the front of my uncle's house to speak of the birth of Yeybona's son whisper that it will soon be the turn of Matunherí's niece and likely successor, me, to bear children.

Of course I will do this, but my time has yet to come. I have not blossomed as quickly as Yeybona has. She is a flower. I am a sea grape, still clinging to the branch.

Because Yeybona is like a sister to me, I went to see the baby immediately. He is a marvel. His skin is smooth and nut brown. Already his eyes are wide open and he looks up at the thatch canopy above his hammock.

My father, who is one of the most skilled craftsmen in Xaraguá, has made the special gift of two small wooden boards and cotton bands to Yeybona, so that she can wrap them around the baby's head to flatten it. At birth all of us must wear these boards. Once they are removed, our foreheads no longer jut out, but slope up in the same way that the tops of our houses slant skyward. This flattening makes us not only more beautiful but also less likely to be overcome by blows to the head when we are older.

Many of the new babies were brought to Matunherí's house so he could see and bless them. In his role as the supreme chief, my uncle is considered the father of all who live in Xaraguá. Our birthright — inherited through my uncle's and my mother's mother — dictates that either Behechio or I are to one day rule Xaraguá, so Behechio and I assist Matunherí in such tasks as greeting the new babies and their parents. It is always a joy to welcome new life to Xaraguá, a pleasure we enjoy with almost every moon.

The name Yeybona and her husband Piragua have chosen for their son is Nahe. Since both Yeybona and Piragua love the sea, and since Piragua's name means "long boat," they have chosen to name their son after the oar we use to row our canoes.

I visited young Nahe again today and in honor of his name whispered in his ear our story of how the sea was made.

Yaya, our supreme ancestor, had an evil son, Yayael, who tried to kill him. His life being in danger, Yaya had no choice but to have his son killed. Since he still loved his son so very much, Yaya put his bones inside a gourd, which he hung from the roof of his house.

One day, missing his son, Yaya told his wife to take down the gourd so he could see the bones. As the wife took down the gourd, fish and sea turtles swam out of it. Yaya's wife was so surprised that she dropped the gourd, and when it broke into pieces, the water that came out was enough to cover all the dry places on the earth.

Nahe seemed to like this story. He waved one little hand in the air as I told it. He will surely hear this story again many times, and in more detail, as he grows older.

HALF MOON, DAY 6

> *The moon never deceives us.*
> *In the sky above us,*
> *There are beings who light their fires at dusk,*
> *Just as we do.*
> *At sunrise, we do not see them,*
> *But they see us*
> *And they marvel at all our trees.*
> *And because the trees please them,*
> *They blow on them.*
> *And when we are hot,*

They blow on us.
And when they are sad,
Their tears fall upon us
And make our flowers grow.
And at sunrise, they put their fires away,
Just as we do.

I sang my new ballad for my father — I call him Baba. Baba, Bibi, and Behechio all say I must perform it for Matunherí at the next feast. Behechio is making a new drum, a *mayohaboa*, to accompany me. This drum is so booming and resonant that our elders call it "the voice of the gods."

HALF MOON, DAY 7

Bibi was bitten by *niguas*, those shrewd little insects that pierce through the skin and lay their eggs in you. It must have happened while we were taking our morning bath. She is suffering from a painful itch.

Almost everyone is bitten by *niguas* on their feet, but my mother has the scourge on both arms. I have seen many in the villages bent over in agony, scratching their feet. At least Bibi does not have to bend to scratch.

Half Moon, Day 8

Bibi has been scratching so much that both her arms are now very swollen. Baba sent for Bayaci, our healer, to examine her. Bayaci has been my mother and father's healer since before I was born. He has great knowledge and will know what to do.

Bayaci ordered a purge for Bibi. She will drink many blended herbs, which will force the *niguas'* poisons out of her body. While he is treating Bibi, as our tradition dictates, Bayaci must take the same remedies he gives her. He also scratches his arms as though he, too, had been bitten by the insects.

I feel very sorry for Bibi, because she seems to be in so much pain. But I am sad for Bayaci as well, who must experience all our illnesses before he can even try to cure us. What difficult work it is to be a healer! I am glad I was born in my family and not Bayaci's, but I don't know what we would ever do without him. How would a family of rulers survive without a family of healers?

Half Moon, Day 9

Bayaci's purge worked. Even though both Bibi and Bayaci were greatly weakened by it, neither is scratching anymore.

Bibi's first act since she regained her strength was to have a new hammock made for herself to replace the one she lay in while she had the itch. That one will be burned in case there are any insect eggs in it.

I watched a duck hunt with my father, brother, and uncle today. In the future, I may sing a ballad about this hunt. To catch the ducks, the duck hunters float empty gourds downstream toward the ducks. Once the ducks are used to seeing the gourds, the hunters put gourds over their heads and, their bodies submerged under water, swim to the ducks. Then the duck hunters reach up to catch the ducks by their legs.

To my ballad, I will add a few riddles:

Are the ducks not aware of the gourd-men?
Do the ducks consult each other about these gourd-men?
Why, after all this time, have the ducks
not learned to flee the gourds?

When I posed these questions to Matunherí, who is the wisest man in Xaraguá, he asked me to remember that the ducks caught by the duck hunters never return to their flock.

Full Moon, Day 11

Bayaci has made amulets for Baba, Bibi, Behechio, and myself, amulets against *niguas* and other pests. These amulets are not like our usual wooden or stone amulets, but are herbs that are meant to repel insects. It is understandable that Bayaci does not want any of us to be sick, as he has to suffer through each and every treatment with us.

Full Moon, Day 12

The tobacco harvest is coming to a close in many of our villages. Several new pipes have been offered to my uncle and he has given many of them to my father. My uncle has also received cigars and chewing tobacco from the nitaíno subchiefs in our villages. He likes to smoke his pipes while he is thinking of answers to difficult problems, and since he must solve many problems, large and small, for the people of Xaraguá, Matunherí thinks and smokes a great deal.

Full Moon, Day 13

Wearing our new herbal amulets against *niguas*, on Matunherí's orders, Behechio and I went fishing with Piragua. My uncle wants Behechio and I to know how everything is done in Xaraguá — from planting to hunting and fishing — so that when either one of us becomes the supreme chief, and people come to us with their problems, we will know what to do.

I was glad to be in Piragua's canoe, in the sea. Though my name comes from the land, I believe myself to be a person of the sea. The sea stories, Yaya and Yayael's especially, are the tales I most like to listen to and recite.

Piragua is a very able fisherman. He pours into the sea a brew made from the *barbasco* plant. The brew makes the fish sleepy and helpless: They float to the surface and we gather as many as we wish into our nets.

FULL MOON, DAY 14

We greeted another group of newborn babies from the villages. Perhaps it is not the tobacco harvest season but the baby harvest season, as we have had more babies born in the villages this season than any other. After Matunherí had welcomed and blessed the babies, to amuse the mothers I told the story of how frogs had come to be.

While playing by the river, a group of small children lost sight of their mothers and began calling "*Toa, Toa*," one of our many words for "mother." The river, which could not safeguard children as well as it could other types of water animals, turned the children into frogs, but even after the children became frogs, they continued to call out "*Toa, Toa*" after their lost mothers.

When telling a story like this, I often ask myself, *What will I be called in the future? Will it be ruler of Xaraguá, or Toa?* As my uncle's days grow close to their end, will he choose me to rule Xaraguá or will he favor Behechio?

All I know is that whether as *cacica* or mother, whatever I do will always be for the good of my people.

FULL MOON, DAY 15

With the final sighting of the full moon, my father and uncle and a group of subchiefs from the villages linger in the plaza near Matunherí's temple before going to sleep. They fill their pipes with fresh tobacco from the harvest and tell stories of past moons: of hurricanes that muddied the rivers and of tempests that demolished entire settlements. They tell of skies filled with clouds that spewed out rain, which flooded their crops and left them with little to eat. They tell of calling on our ancestors to save them, and of how, just when they thought they were all going to die, the rains would stop and the moon would come out and they would begin a new season of planting and they would think of the moon as a marble garden that is always replenishing itself and they would immediately feel more hopeful.

Listening to Baba, Matunherí, and the subchiefs, I carve on a flattened rock as round as the moon the entire realm of Quisqueya, of which Xaraguá is only one part. Quisqueya, which we also call Ayiti and Bohio, being a hand and each separate territory, a finger.

On the island of Quisqueya, there is also Maguá, the realm of valleys and plains, and Higüey, a populated region where food grows easily. There is Marién, which is carefully sheltered between high mountain ranges and the sea and is full of gold and copper mines. Then there is, aside from Xaraguá, my most favorite region, Maguana, ruled by the handsome Caonabó, whose name means "Ruler of the House of Gold."

My uncle has taken Behechio and me to visit all the other chiefs of Quisqueya and their territories, and many of the chiefs have also come to Xaraguá. This, so that harmony can be maintained whether my uncle rules Xaraguá or Behechio or I do.

Matunherí's moonlit gathering particularly brings to mind the face of Caonabó, the ruler of Maguana. When Behechio, Matunherí, and a large group of our people visited with him in Maguana, he arranged an *areito* in our honor, a feast of singing and dancing and ball games that lasted for several moons. As we were leaving Maguana, Chief Caonabó offered Matunherí several high-backed ceremonial chairs, all carved in stone and adorned with seashells and gold. He also gifted us with many beautiful ceramic vessels and strong cotton hammocks. He is a most generous chief and I hope to see him again.

LAST QUARTER MOON, DAY 16

Baba organized a ball game after dusk, a *batey* by the light of the moon. Behechio caused much laughter among us players when he let the ball touch his hands on several occasions, missing his legs and lean backside. The group Behechio was leading lost the ball game. The group I was part of won.

Again my thoughts return to Chief Caonabó of Maguana. I wish Matunherí would decide to have us visit him again.

LAST QUARTER MOON, DAY 17

The guava growers' children, whose work it is to protect the fields from the birds, toil very hard as the guava harvesting season approaches. Like us, the birds love these sweet fruits, and who can fault them?

Our elders tell us that our dead also like to eat guava and can even transform themselves into the fruit at night.

When the children see a flock of birds flying over their fields, they wave their arms wildly as though they, too, wish they could fly.

I went with Yeybona to witness Nahe's first swim. Like a toad he glides on the river, his mother's hand firmly under him while he takes quick, short breaths that help keep him afloat.

After Yeybona and Nahe left, I stayed on the beach until nightfall, watching the sun fade from the sky and the moon and the stars appear. It was then that I noticed the feeble light of dimmed torches and heard the faint sounds of drums slowly heading toward the sea. I am sure now that it was them, the Night Marchers, ghosts of old warriors, walking from their burial grounds to the freedom of the sea.

I kept my head down, for if you ever see Night Marchers on their stroll from death to the afterlife, the elders say, they will carry you with them into the sea. And since I am not yet ready for the afterlife, I simply I listened to the faint sound of their drums and waited for their lanterns' shadows to disappear before I ran home and slipped into a not-so-peaceful slumber.

I told Behechio that I heard the Night Marchers on the beach last night. He said many people think they hear Night Marchers when what they're probably listening to is the sound of a distant village feast.

I was certain it was them, I told him. But he said he was playing his drum last night with Matunherí's musicians and this is probably what I heard.

"Did you look at them?" he asked.

"I thought if you looked at them, you could die," I said.

"Which is why no one who's claimed to have seen them is to be believed."

"What about the faint lights slowly moving toward the sea?" I asked.

"The stars," he said. "Moving in the sky."

I couldn't argue with him anymore. But I am sure of what I heard and felt. He was simply jealous. I had been in the presence of Night Marchers and he never had.

GUAVA PLANTING SEASON
FIRST QUARTER MOON, DAY 1

> *Again we plant guavas*
> *After an abundant harvest.*
> *Sacred fruit,*

Loved by both the living
And the dead,
May you blossom quickly.

FIRST QUARTER MOON, DAY 2

I have grown taller in the last period. I am even taller now than Behechio. So with the first sighting of the next full moon, I will have my haircutting celebration. This is the second time my hair will be cut since I was born. The first time was when I had just begun walking and I can't even remember it now. This time when my uncle uses his ceremonial ax to cut my hair from waist length to my shoulders, I will become a woman.

My uncle has ordered Cuybio to make a special headband and skirt for me to wear to the haircutting ceremony. Bibi and I are making some neck, arm, and foot adornments. I will also be expected to perform my first dance as a woman. Matunherí has put some of his wives at my disposal, the ones most skillful at dancing. I have not consulted them because I want to create my own dance.

Behechio has arranged for the most elaborate ball game for the feast in my honor. Matunherí has also instructed that there be some mock fighting to entertain our visitors. He did not say who the visitors might be. Could Chief Caonabó be among them?

First Quarter Moon, Day 4

Bibi and Baba have consulted Matunherí about which chiefs will be at my ceremony. Almost all the chiefs of Quisqueya will come or will send emissaries. As one who might one day rule Xaraguá, I will receive many wonderful gifts, as each of the caciques tries to outdo the others.

Behechio has asked Matunherí whether Chief Caonabó will come or send a replacement. We have learned that Chief Caonabó will come himself with many important people from his territory. Behechio is concerned about Chief Caonabó's visit not for my sake but his. Behechio is actively seeking a wife now and he wants to personally consult with all the chiefs about this.

First Quarter Moon, Day 5

I know now what my dance will be. It will be a dance of gratitude to the ancestors and to Matunherí, and then to my parents. Even though they surrendered Behechio and me to Matunherí to be raised as future rulers of Xaraguá, they did not abandon us but remained close by to help guide us toward our destinies. Bibi and Baba's instruction has been as crucial to me as my uncle's, but out of respect for Matunherí's superior position I will apply many more movements in my gratitude dance to him.

I asked Baba to make the masks for my dance. He has always been the one to craft my masks in the past, for both large and small feasts. Even with Matunherí's best artisans at my disposal, I would never have anyone but Baba make my dancing masks. He always carves them just as I would myself.

HALF MOON, DAY 6

Cuybio has created the most radiant attire for my ceremony. Around my forehead I will wear a cotton ribbon dipped in hemp and scented herbs speckled with coral and gold.

Even though I am not accepting help from Matunherí's wives, I gladly accepted his offer to have his musicians accompany me during my dance.

Baba has already completed the masks, too. They are the best he has ever done. As I requested, each mask shows my face at different ages, from the time I was an infant, like Yeybona and Piragua's Nahe, to this moment. I will dance as a baby, then as a girl, then, with my own face, I will perform my gratitude dance. I have begun training with the masks, going deep into the woods with Matunherí's musicians, where no one can hear or see us.

One additional reason to be extremely grateful to my beloved Baba: He crafted those masks so quickly, without asking me to sit with him so he could re-create my face. It must be that he knows so well the face of his golden flower.

HALF MOON, DAY 7

I was training for my dance in the woods when Behechio came to find me, saying that my uncle wished to speak to me immediately. Matunherí had heard that I'd refused the counsel of his wives and he wanted to know what kind of dance I would perform at the ceremony. I told him it was one of my own creation. He told me that my little dances were sufficient for our villagers, but we were going to have important people at the ceremony and I was to be sure not to shame him or Xaraguá. Even though I had only one of the masks with me, the one of me as an infant, he insisted that I perform my dance for him. I had no choice but to obey for he is not only my uncle but also the supreme leader of Xaraguá. Thankfully, he had no objections. Now that both he and Behechio have seen part of my dance, I must change it so that it might still be a good surprise.

HALF MOON, DAY 8

The worst curse: I have been bitten by *niguas,* and on my feet. My dancing feet. In the excitement of preparing for the ceremony, I had stopped wearing the amulets Bayaci had made me, and now I will pay a grave price.

Bibi called for Bayaci immediately, asking him for a quick cure that would prevent my feet from swelling further. The cure is this: Along with the purge of herbs, I must stop eating in order to purify myself. I was to do a cleansing fast on the eve of my ceremony, anyway, but now my fast will last longer, and I wonder if I will have the strength to participate in my own ceremony if I am starved and weak.

HALF MOON, DAY 9

I fear I will be a corpse as I travel toward womanhood, my body stiff and thin, my legs as large as tree trunks. Cuybio has made me some wide ribbons to wear around my feet to hide the swelling. Will these ribbons be sufficient? Cuybio is very skilled at crafting things with cotton, but can he save my honor? Xaraguá's honor?

I pray to the ancestors for an immediate cure. If they truly wish for me to become a woman, I will be cured. If they mean for me to remain a girl, then I will hobble through my ceremony and I will not dance.

Half Moon, Day 10

It is the eve of my ceremony. With the purges and the massages and the fast, my feet have grown a bit smaller. I even left my hammock, where I have been resting, to walk around my uncle's courtyard, taking very careful steps. I still feel as though the little pests are at war in my feet, but *niguas* or no *niguas* our guests have already begun to arrive and my ceremony must proceed as planned.

Full Moon, Day 12

It was a marvelous ceremony. At sunrise, Bayaci woke me to examine my legs and they were as flat as before. Only the tiny marks remained where the pests had bitten into my skin. I thanked the ancestors with great joy. They must have visited me during the night and removed all the poison from my feet so I could dance in their honor. (Bayaci's very tight, herb-soaked dressing helped as well.)

Bayaci was glad I was better. He had been worried — though he never showed it — that my uncle would blame or even punish him for not curing me in time for the ceremony.

Once Bayaci saw that I was well, though still a bit weak, he insisted that I be fed a plate of pineapples and salted fish to build up my strength.

After I ate, Bibi weaved my hair into a long braid, which hung like a rope down my back. My uncle was then carried on his highest chair to visit me, offering me a figurine of a frog — a special amulet, or *zemi*, that had belonged to my grandmother.

After Matunherí left, Bibi helped me cover my whole body in red paste made from the crimson-seeded *roucou* plant, then I put on my beautiful attire from Cuybio. I no longer needed the wide cotton ribbons for my ankles, but I wore them for good fortune when the time came to walk from my parents' house to the plaza, where everyone was waiting.

Matunherí was carried at the head of the procession on his ceremonial chair. He sounded a conch shell; Behechio followed behind him, then me. When I reached the plaza, it was full not only with our guests from far away but also with the villagers, who had come to watch.

Matunherí spoke a few words, calling on the ancestors to stand with me on this day and for the rest of my life. Then a ceremonial cloth and stone were brought forward. Bibi lowered the cloth for me to lie on and Baba lay the stone down where I was to put my head.

Letting my braid slip behind the stone, I looked up at the sky and waited for my uncle to drop his ax. Up above me, the sun was bright, its rays bouncing off everything, including the blade of my uncle's ax when he raised it from his side, preparing to strike in my direction.

For a moment I feared my uncle's hands would tremble and he would let the blade fall on my neck. Then I had one of those sensations that the ancestors might be speaking to me, and what they seemed to be telling me was that I might be in a situation like this again one day, but in that future moment something painful might be done to my neck.

There was no time for me to think further on this for just as quickly as my uncle's ax was raised and lowered, my head felt lighter and my hair was gone.

My uncle bent down and raised my fallen braid for all to see. Sounds of approval rose from the villagers, and just like that I was disjoined from my childhood, the way a baby is separated from its mother when its umbilical chord is cut.

Matunherí reached down again and raised me from the ground. I felt a bit dizzy and couldn't see very well at first, perhaps because my eyes had been facing the sky and the floating white clouds. Then Matunherí embraced me, as did Behechio and my parents.

A chair, which had been especially made for the ceremony, one with a slightly lower back than my uncle's, was placed in the middle of the courtyard, where I sat to greet my guests and receive my gifts.

I was offered many bracelets and necklaces made of silver and gold and others made from sea rocks, shark teeth, seashells, and clay. I received extravagant headdresses from the chiefs and their emissaries, and belts embellished with dye and feathers. There were also large gifts of food: baskets of fish, whole iguanas, turtles, and manatee, peppers, peanuts, sweet potatoes, plantains, yams, corn, beans, squash, bananas, guavas, pineapples, and papayas.

Many of the chiefs had brought their daughters and nieces with them hoping that Behechio would choose one or several of them as wives. After greeting many of these young women who might one day be my sisters, I finally came face-to-face once more with Chief Caonabó. He looked like the great chief he was, adorned in his large breastplate of copper, silver, and gold and a headdress made from the feathers of birds unlike any we have in Xaraguá. He was carrying a well-carved scepter decorated with translucent stones. His hair was long in the back, almost as long as mine had been before my ceremony, but it was neatly cut in the front, framing his golden bronze face. His gift to me was a cage full of those birds from which the feathers of his headdress seem to have been pulled, birds for which we have no name here. The birds were each as bright as a rainbow, with every feather a different color. Even the servants who were collecting the gifts on my behalf seemed puzzled as to what might be done with these types of birds. Should they be kept for decoration or should they be killed and eaten? They were so beautiful I could not think of ever having them killed.

As the servants accepted the cage of birds, Chief Caonabó leaned toward me and whispered in my ear, "I hope you will fly from here like these birds and come to Maguana."

I asked him why he would give me birds he was so certain would fly from here and return to Maguana.

He said he was hoping I would feel so much pity for the birds that I would let them out of their cage and when they flew away would follow them.

Before I could ask any more questions, he turned and walked away, crossing the courtyard to rejoin my uncle.

I soon lost sight of him, having to pay attention to my other guests and exchange a few words with them. There were more gifts and good wishes, then it was time to eat.

The meats and fishes were grilled and roasted on a tall *barbacoa* stand. As one who had been ill and fasting for some time, I wanted to eat every piece. Still, everyone, including myself, ate their fill and, after a short rest, either watched or participated in mock fights and ball games.

As the sun set, it was my turn to dance. My uncle's musicians were marvelous, for even though we had stopped training for the dance when I was bitten by the *niguas*, no one watching would have ever known it. The musicians followed my every step, adjusting quickly when I surprised them with unfamiliar movements. My feet, too, were as buoyant as the breeze and it was as though the *niguas* were helping rather than hindering me.

I directed my movements at the sky and the sea when I was thanking the ancestors, then at Matunherí when I was thanking him, then at my parents when I thanked them. In the end, I added some new movements, thanking all the high chiefs and subchiefs who had brought or sent me such wonderful gifts. I wanted to thank Chief Caonabó in particular for the beautiful birds he had brought me, but I did not think it wise to show too much interest in him, as it might make it harder for my uncle to claim a large marriage price for me.

When I was done with my dance, I could tell that everyone was pleased, including my uncle. Bibi and Baba looked delighted, even though Behechio appeared a bit jealous.

There was more singing, dancing, and spinning of tales until sunrise, when the guests began to leave, the chiefs and their emissaries making their way to the beach where, along with their large parties, they boarded their canoes and began their journey back home.

I lost sight of Chief Caonabó soon after my dance. By the time I inquired about him, Behechio told me he was already gone.

Full Moon, Day 13

I am no longer to have my morning baths with Bibi but now must bathe with my uncle's wives, who each has a servant to wash her. On Matunherí's orders, I, too, must have someone wash me. It must not appear that the cacique's wives are treated better than one who might one day rule Xaraguá.

I will miss my sunrise baths with Bibi, but we both

knew this time would come. Still, I did not expect these changes to make me so sad, even if these are the steps I must take to rule one day. To keep from crying while the servants slap the cleansing plants on my back in the river at sunrise, I remind myself that I will still be with Bibi at the communal meals and other occasions.

There is now so much to learn in preparation for my rule, so much to get accustomed to. Behechio, who has never been as attached to our parents as I am, says that I must act as though I am already cacica, thinking only of Xaraguá as my mother and my father.

Full Moon, Day 14

A wife has been found for Behechio. He seems overjoyed about this and is already making preparations for his marriage. She is not one of the many young women who came to my ceremony. He has never met her and neither have I. She is someone my uncle has chosen, the youngest daughter of one of the subchiefs of another region.

I asked Behechio about his future wife, wanting to learn as much about her as I could in order to prepare a proper welcome. He knew no more about her than I did. Each time he tried to ask my uncle about her, my uncle reacted in a brusque way, as though Behechio was challenging his choice, so Behechio stopped asking. I consoled him by saying that whoever his wife is, she will probably be good for Xaraguá and will earn us an ally in one chief or another. Otherwise my uncle would have never chosen her.

FULL MOON, DAY 15

Behechio's intended is to come soon so that they can be married. If he is to have a wife before long, then how much further behind can I be?

I pray there will never be a battle between Behechio and myself for authority over Xaraguá, but I must accept that should he marry, he will stay here among our people and close to our uncle, but should I marry — as I eventually will — I will have to leave Xaraguá.

In light of Behechio's marriage, I have decided that I will only marry on the condition that the status of the man I am joined with is equal to my own, one with powers that are equal to those I must surrender here in Xaraguá.

LAST QUARTER MOON, DAY 16

A riddle to myself:

> *Why would I consider leaving Xaraguá*
> *for Chief Caonabó's Maguana?*

Response:

> *My marriage to Chief Caonabó would strengthen the*
> *already agreeable ties between our two peoples.*
> *My husband would be a cacique*
> *and I would help him rule.*

Another riddle to myself:

> *Why would I stay in Xaraguá,*
> *even if I remain unmarried?*

Response:

> *In Xaraguá, I can rule in my own name or with*
> *my brother. In Maguana, I can only be the wife,*
> *or one of the wives, of the supreme chief.*

LAST QUARTER MOON, DAY 17

It is night. I am sad and — I must confess — lovelorn. I cannot sleep. I have with me the amulet my uncle gave me, the one that once belonged to my grandmother, the last cacica of Xaraguá. I treasure this amulet in the shape of a frog, as much as I cherish the legends told about my grandmother. Made in the form of a fast and agile water beast, it was the symbol of her reign, as she considered herself the *toa*, the mother, of all her people.

Our elders tell stories of how my grandmother ruled by these dictums:

Never attack unless attacked.

Hunt only what is needed.

Protect our young at any cost.

There are no stories told of my grandmother feeling amorous and downhearted, as I am now, yearning for other chiefs from other territories, nor of her ever considering abandoning her birthright. Even though she married and produced heirs, it is said that there was only room in my grandmother's heart for one great love, and that was Xaraguá.

LATER

I grow more and more sad as the night wears on. What's worse, I still cannot sleep. The birds Chief Caonabó gave me have been kept behind my uncle's house in a corner of the courtyard, close to my hammock. At night they make the most melodious sound, lulling me to sleep. It is a sound between moaning and laughing, a sound that reminds me of the demeanor of Chief Caonabó himself. If one listens to the sound with longing in one's heart, it can make one sad, but if one listens with joy, it can easily make one blissful.

Since we still have had no word from Chief Caonabó about me, I can only listen to his birds with sadness, their moans and chirps tearing at my heart. So under this final thread of the last quarter moon, I opened the cage and shooed Chief Caonabó's birds away.

At first they seemed hesitant to fly, as though the night might hinder their journey, but finally one fluttered off, then another, until the cage was empty and they were all gone.

I don't know what made me sadder, the empty cage or the birds' flight. But at last I will be free of all reminders of Chief Caonabó. Let his birds return to him and let him see that I have not followed them.

YUCCA HARVEST SEASON
First Quarter Moon, Day 1

It is time to harvest the yucca, a strong root that sustains us all.

Of all the harvests, the yucca harvest is the one we profit most from. Not only do we eat yuccas roasted and boiled, but from our yucca harvest we make cassava bread, *cassareep* — a delicious sauce that often makes me lick my fingers — and *uicu*, a yucca wine greatly favored by my uncle and father and now Behechio.

Sometimes I ask myself what we would do if there were no yucca. Perhaps we would die of hunger, just as we would die of sickness if there were no healers.

I have continued to grow taller these past seasons. Bibi, Baba, and Matunherí all concur that I am even taller than my grandmother is said to have been at this same cycle in her life. Perhaps I shall be the tallest cacica of Xaraguá.

Though my grandmother died before I was born, I always feel that she is with me in her death. Perhaps it is she who is guiding my destiny from the land of the ancestors, making me grow and *feel* stronger with each passing moon.

I often have the sensation that my grandmother would like to rule again from the land of the dead and will choose to do it through me. Perhaps she has made me superior in height so that in my own body I can bear both her carriage and mine and still have enough courage to look any chief in the eye and fight at his side if needed — or against him if necessary.

This past season, Behechio has taken no less than a handful of wives — that is, five in total. He has his own household, where he resides with all of them, and he spends most of his time there.

I thought I would gain sisters among my brother's wives, but this has not been the case. He has kept them all to himself; I only see them at meals, ceremonies, and dances.

I speak to Behechio daily when my uncle calls us together to watch him exercise his duties, presiding over the morning meal, demanding accounts from the sub-chiefs, and other such matters.

Behechio has told me that he would like to have more wives. Young women are sent for him to consider all the time and he enjoys choosing from them or sending them away.

Though my uncle has traded goods and continues to share a friendship with Chief Caonabó, the chief appears to have expressed no further interest in me. There are still others who would have me, but I do not want them and I will not yield from my position, even if my chilling omen at the haircutting ceremony comes true and my uncle lowers his ax on my neck.

Bibi and Baba and I went to watch a group of villagers harvest the yucca, just as we used to do when I was younger. While sitting under the large silk cotton tree near the yucca field, they told me that Chief Caonabó is interested in having me as his wife, but my uncle is not yet willing to release me. Matunherí wants to be certain that Behechio is skilled enough to rule Xaraguá before he can let me leave for Maguana.

All at once I was filled with many emotions. I felt a great deal of love for my mother and father, who knew I was suffering and wanted to relieve my pain. I felt honored that Matunherí did not want to let me go. I felt, once again, a warmth in my heart for Chief Caonabó, and then felt pity for Behechio, because all he seems interested in anymore are his wives.

FIRST QUARTER MOON, DAY 5

At dusk, Matunherí called me to sing a ballad for him and his wives. It seems that one of them had requested it. She did not want to hear one of the ballads we have inherited from our elders, but one of my own creation.

I almost refused this request, for it is difficult to sing with no preparation, but I did not want to displease him. With Matunherí, there are some moments when I feel like his successor and others when I feel like a servant, but I am certain that he is trying to instruct me in many ways, is helping me learn the ancient lesson that, though servants never rule, rulers must serve.

Behechio had a loud quarrel with one of his wives. It appears that she traded some mortars and pestles without speaking to him first. Bibi and Baba are usually the ones who trade the mortars and pestles on my uncle's behalf. Behechio threatened to return his wife to her village, but both Matunherí and Baba intervened and she will stay.

Later that night, I found the wife Behechio had quarreled with crying in the courtyard behind Matunherí's house. Her name is Yaruba. She no longer wants to stay in Xaraguá, but would like to return to her village.

I asked her what village she was from. She motioned toward the seas as if to indicate a place far in the distance and stopped sobbing long enough to whisper that she was from a village in Maguana.

My heart began to beat faster and I asked her, "Is it Maguana, where Caonabó is chief?"

She shook her head, signaling yes.

In Maguana, her uncle is a subchief under Chief Caonabó. Her uncle barters with Matunherí for the special wood from which we make our mortars and pestles, which we then trade in other territories. Yaruba had traded some special mortars and pestles on which she had carved messages to her uncle saying that she wanted to return home.

There was no question of her returning home without causing some disagreement between our two territories, which is why Baba and Bibi and my uncle had made her stay. Now she was unhappy that she had fallen out of favor with Behechio, whom she did not like, anyway.

I felt so sad for Yaruba because she was in a situation that I could easily find myself in, living far from her family and her people and missing them very much. I told her to take heart, that I would speak to Matunherí on her behalf and maybe he would send her back.

She replied that she had already made up her mind to leave, that she would return home soon. It was only a matter of means until she found some way to escape.

It was brave of her to confide in me since I could have gone to my uncle or to Behechio and denounced her, but I think somehow she could tell that I wouldn't betray her.

To ease her sadness, I asked her to tell me what she loved most about Maguana. I thought this would make her feel like she was on a visit there and at the same time give me a chance to learn more about her land.

She said Maguana was the most golden place, with so much gold strewn over so many parts of the land that from the sky Maguana might look like another sun. She said the supreme cacique, Chief Caonabó, ruled with kindness though he was a strong warrior and able to protect their people against invaders, especially the Kalinas from across the seas.

Her favorite place in Maguana was a bluff overlooking the sea, where she could watch the trade canoes row out at sunrise and in again at sunset.

Back when she was in Maguana, she said, she'd thought she wanted to leave, but now she wished she never had.

We parted with a squeeze of the hand.

I know Behechio. He is unforgiving and may never speak to Yaruba again for the rest of his life. Even if she remains in his house, he will quickly replace her with someone younger and more docile.

I ran back to her and told her to meet me again at sunrise. Perhaps we could go to one of our bluffs and watch the canoes come in and out or we could go for a stroll near the yucca field to watch the yucca growers harvest the yucca and then squeeze the poisonous *hyen* juices out of the roots to make cassava bread.

She said she had already seen that, had even participated in the yucca harvest against Behechio's wishes.

I told her perhaps we would find some other activity that would please her even more.

She said we would see.

Once again we said good-bye and began walking away

from each other. She turned around and said she enjoyed my ballads. She had heard me singing for my uncle's wives.

Suddenly I had one of my sensations that perhaps she was ill or hiding something from everyone, including me. Then what it was became as clear as daylight, and I quickly ran back to her.

I asked her if she was with child and she shook her head, indicating yes.

I asked if Behechio knew.

She said no. No one knew.

She asked how I could tell. Could everyone tell?

I didn't know how to explain, so I told her I had a gift for such things, a kind of skill that Bibi said I had inherited from my grandmother.

She shook her head and smiled. She asked what else I could see in her future.

I said I could see nothing more at the moment. I simply had that one revelation that she was with child. Then I began to plead with her. She must not escape. She must stay with us. Behechio has no heirs. This would be his first child.

We heard someone coming. We thought it might be Behechio or one of his other wives, but it was a servant from Behechio's household, looking for Yaruba.

Yaruba told me she was tired and would come looking for me at sunrise so we could talk further. Then she and the servant walked away together, blending into the night.

HALF MOON, DAY 7

Yaruba is dead. Behechio found a half gourd of the poisonous juices from the yucca roots beneath her hammock. He seemed very troubled and talked to no one after he announced her death.

I have decided not to tell him that Yaruba was with child. This would only make the situation more difficult to bear. It seems plain to me now that Behechio had cared for Yaruba, as much as he cared for any of his wives. He had only quarreled with her because he did not want to disturb the usual order of things in my uncle's and his household. Had he let Yaruba return home, it would have been seen as an insult to her uncle and a sign of rejection of all of Maguana's women.

I asked Behechio's permission to take charge of Yaruba's burial and he obliged. I know of several small caves on a bluff overlooking our seas and thought it would be fitting to inter her there. From those caves, she could see not only the trade canoes row in and out but also, perhaps, a faint silhouette of her village in Maguana.

HALF MOON, DAY 8

We interred Yaruba in one of the caves by the sea. My uncle was present, as was Behechio and his other wives, along with Bibi and Baba and many of the subchiefs from our villages and the yucca growers whose roots Yaruba had taken from the harvest to poison herself.

What a sad fate, to die alone, so far from one's home!

I ask myself a riddle for which perhaps there is no answer: *Is it truly better to die than to suffer among the living?*

HALF MOON, DAY 9

Behechio has not left his house since Yaruba died. Understanding him as well as I do, I know he must be tormented by the idea that something he said or did to Yaruba could have led her to poison herself.

I am terribly distressed that I can't console him as he refuses to see anyone at all.

Our elders tell this story about the land of the dead:

There is a part of Quisqueya that we do not count among its five territories because it is the land of the dead. Though our dead remain in this territory, Soraya, from dawn to dusk, at night they visit with the living. And as the dead move among us, the only difference between them and ourselves is that they have no navels.

HALF MOON, DAY 10

I finally went to Behechio's house, against his orders, to speak with him. After a long silence, he told me he feared that Yaruba would return from the land of the dead in the form of another woman to punish him.

I reminded him that all he must do when he chooses his next wife is see if she has a navel.

Now I fear that my brother will take on many more wives, simply because they *have* navels.

I said this to him.

He smiled.

It was good to see him smile. He, too, has been acting like an inhabitant of the land of the dead. I would have thought he was dead, were it not for his navel.

FULL MOON, DAY 11

I went to the mouth of the cave where Yaruba is interred. Behechio was there, sitting at the entrance, watching the sea. A riddle for Behechio:

> *Why must we wait until people are dead*
> *to realize how much we valued them?*

Behechio has been going to the mouth of Yaruba's cave every sunrise. He does not leave until dusk. I go with him.

He does not talk, but simply looks at the sea. I am so afraid for him. I fear that he will throw himself in the sea.

FULL MOON, DAY 12

An answer to my riddle about suffering: Behechio supplied it for me as we sat at the mouth of the cave. He is talking again, but only a few words at a time.

Yes, there are moments when one might feel that it is better to die than to suffer, he said, but we must always let these moments pass, especially if we are to rule Xaraguá one day. (I sensed he was talking as much to himself as to me.)

The answer to the other riddle I posed to him:

Why must we wait until people are dead
to realize how much we valued them?

Because whether we are *nitaínos* or *naborías*, whether we were born of high or low stature, he said, we still lack the wisdom of our ancestors, who have been through both life and death.

Yaruba is an ancestor now, I told him, she is wiser than she used to be and certainly wiser than we are. Perhaps she will help guide us, like our grandmother and others who have preceded us.

The biggest lesson that Yaruba taught him, Behechio

said, or has reminded him of, is to be kinder to people who have left their own land to come to ours, especially if they come with hope and enthusiasm.

What would he do now? I asked him. Would he spend the rest of his life at the mouth of this cave? Like our ancestor Mácocael, who must stand guard at the mouths of the caves and, when he comes out into the sunlight, turns into stone?

This would be his last visit to the cave, he said. He had been too distracted by his wives for too long. Now he would love only Xaraguá.

FULL MOON, DAY 13

Our elders tell this story about our ancestor Mácocael. Long ago, when we were night creatures, like the bats who make their homes inside caves, it was Mácocael's duty to stand outside the caves and close the cave doors when the sun came up. Mácocael performed this duty admirably and with diligence for many moons until one morning he did not come back inside. Fearful that the sun had carried him away, the elders inside the cave locked the cave and left Mácocael outside. Surprised by the sun, which had come up sooner than usual, Mácocael turned to stone.

I had feared that, like Mácocael, Behechio would turn to stone, or at least that his heart would, but it seems that, in spite of himself, his heart has softened, if not toward his living wives then toward Yaruba. I went to the mouth of Yaruba's cave today and, true to his promise, Behechio was not there. He was again at my uncle's side, seeing to his duties. I, too, must return to my duties, and with the same dedication that Behechio is beginning to display once again.

FULL MOON, DAY 14

A common disaster has struck! Several of our villages were attacked by the Kalinas, our enemies from across the seas. They took much of our newly harvested yucca, many of our men, and even more of our women, who they will force to bear their children. Though our villagers fought bravely, they were not as strong as the invaders, who are trained warriors.

When he heard of the attacks, my uncle simply ordered the carving of a special *zemi* in the shape of a serpent, to call on our ancestors to protect our villages. (I myself would prefer to find the Kalinas, destroy them, and leave them for *real* serpents to eat.)

Our elders tell us that for as long as we've been in

Quisqueya, Kalinas have come from across the seas to plunder our gardens and take our people away. I wish our elders could tell us how to battle the Kalinas and, better still, defeat them.

I despise the Kalinas! They pillage and steal. I do understand wars and battles, but I don't understand seizing unearned property and innocent people. I never will!

I had a terrible dream that I was captured and hanged during one of the Kalinas' attacks. I have dreamed of many things that have come to be, like that Yeybona would be with child even before she conceived Nahe, or that a certain group would win at a game. None of my dreams has frightened me as much as the one of the Kalinas taking me away, tying a rope around my neck, and hanging me from a tree.

Of this I am certain: The Kalinas will not stop attacking us unless we can fight like them. When I rule Xaraguá, I will make certain that all our people become as strong and fierce as the Kalina warriors.

Matunherí, Behechio, and I met with many of the sub-chiefs from the villages, who came to tell us of the extent of the Kalinas' attacks. Many more women were taken than at first thought, reducing the population of one small village to men alone. This makes me so angry that I could eat their flesh, like the Kalinas are said to do with those of the men they capture.

At night I cannot sleep, thinking of all the children whose mothers were taken from our villages. All of these children's houses must now be like the river's edge, where little frogs cry out "*toa, toa*" late into the night.

LAST QUARTER MOON, DAY 17

My uncle has chosen to isolate himself in the prayer house so he can speak to our ancestors and let them advise him on what to do about the Kalinas. Like me, he is worried that the next Kalina attack will not be against our villagers but against our household.

This has always been the fear of caciques and cacicas, even in my grandmother's time, Bibi said at the sunrise meal, from which my uncle was absent.

Rulers throughout Quisqueya have always feared that their households would be attacked, so along with the best servants, they surround themselves with the most skilled fighters, men who know the ways of the Kalinas and could at least frighten them.

Baba also joined in our talk, reassuring Behechio and myself that the same men who participate in our mock battles with clubs, spears, and bows and arrows could easily defend my uncle's household against the Kalinas.

Rather than feel more protected, I thought of how unguarded the villagers, who don't have this gathering of strong fighters surrounding them, must be.

Why not train fighters who will protect all of Xaraguá, and position them on the beaches to watch for invaders the way Mácocael watched for the sun at the mouths of the caves? Why don't all of us become fighters, like the Kalinas?

Behechio agrees with me, but Bibi and Baba think we should let Matunherí rule as he wishes.

Later, as the two who might one day be responsible for Xaraguá, Behechio and I spoke alone. We have decided that we will consult Matunherí about doing some things we haven't done before to protect our people against the Kalinas.

Behechio and I had some of the same thoughts: walls around our villages; fishermen with spears to guard the rivers and ocean entryways; more trained fighters, so that each village has its own group of combatants.

Behechio was roused by the possibility of discovering a solution that, for some reason, no one had thought of before. It was the first time *I* thought I would feel at ease living in Xaraguá under my brother's rule, the first time I realized that he would make an excellent chief, with or without my help.

LAST QUARTER MOON, DAY 18

My uncle has resurfaced. While in the prayer house, he fasted and prayed and sat thinking for uninterrupted periods of time.

The first thing he did after coming out was gather the subchiefs in the courtyard and command that more spears and clubs and bows and arrows be constructed by the villagers so that they'd be better prepared to defend themselves. Some of the fighters who guard us will gather selected groups from our villages to train them in the Kalinas' war methods.

Though we will not cross the seas into the Kalinas' territories to fight them, my uncle says, if they come to our lands and attempt to destroy us, we must do to them the same as they would do to us.

Matunherí has given his blessing for Behechio and me to train with his fighters, so that we will be among those to defend Xaraguá if necessary.

Before we began our training, one of the oldest fighters told us that our grandmother had also trained with him to fight against invaders.

Like many of the rulers of her time, my grandmother had a frequent dream that clothed men would come from lands much farther away than those of the Kalinas and would cause us great pain.

Her whole life, the old man said, my grandmother had trained and waited for these clothed men. He himself was grateful the clothed men never came. Trying to defend ourselves against the Kalinas is difficult enough.

THE CORN HARVEST/RAINY SEASON
FIRST QUARTER MOON, DAY 1

Our elders tell this story about corn: It grows on the moon, so we must always plant and harvest it during a new moon. Some of our elders also say that the first people who walked the earth grew out of the corn and thus we are all children of the corn.

It is a cool and breezy day. The wind is blowing through the trees, forcing them to shed both fruits and leaves. It will be harder to harvest the corn, but harvest it we must, before the rains come in full force and drown the stalks.

We have all been staying inside, except the corn growers, who must endure the elements to continue their work. Adding to our troubles, my poor uncle has been ill. He has a cough and chills that refuse to go away, no matter what his healers do.

I can't bear to see Matunherí suffer. Behechio, Bibi, Baba, and I sit with him for long stretches, watching him battle for every breath. It is doubly painful seeing the healers echo his illness as they try all they can to find effective remedies for him.

As Matunherí's condition has not improved in some time, the *bohiti* have resorted to their most potent strategies, blackening their faces with ashes and feeding him a ground-charcoal paste to cleanse his insides. They have bellowed healing ballads and lit ceremonial torches so that the healing spirits can find him more easily. They have massaged every part of his body to force his afflictions out through his skin, covered him in manatee hide to sweat him, and made him lie unclad in his hammock to cool him off. Nothing has worked.

Behechio has commissioned several healing amulets

for the prayer house, where Matunherí is carried regularly to reflect and pray. Bibi, Baba, and I have carved a few of the healing figurines ourselves, breathing into them now and then as though they were my uncle, for whose life we would easily trade our own.

First Quarter Moon, Day 2

With Matunherí being ill, Behechio and I have had to assume more and more of his responsibilities. At the sunrise and sunset meals, we are the ones who receive the subchiefs from our villages and listen to their accounts from the territory.

Though we have not had a Kalinas raid since the yucca harvest — perhaps the Kalinas have turned their attention to other territories — we are now better prepared should one come.

Not only are Behechio and I trained for battle but each of our villages has its own group of skilled combatants. Because of the rainy weather, walls have not yet been built around the villages, but this is something we hope to accomplish soon after the sun resurfaces.

Though he is still ill, my uncle forced himself out of his hammock to sit in one of his ceremonial chairs and smoke his favorite pipe. This is his way of reminding us that he is still the supreme ruler of Xaraguá, regardless of how many of his activities are now being performed by Behechio and me.

Matunherí received many of the subchiefs, then called for his weaver, Cuybio, whom he asked to make him some new head and body coverings, as he has grown quite thin.

Music could be heard coming from my uncle's house at sunset, a different sort of sound than the ballads his healers had been singing. It was livelier music, full of flutes, drums, conch shells, and maracas. Matunherí's musicians were making music that would even make the stars want to dance.

As future rulers of Xaraguá, Behechio and I went to the prayer house to ask the ancestors to heal my uncle. In the prayer house were several of the healing carvings

Behechio had commissioned, many of which I had made with my own hands.

Behechio and I spent most of our time before three ceremonial stones that Matunherí had placed at the center of the prayer house. Of the three stones, one was to help bring good harvests to Xaraguá, the second to help our women bear children without pain, and the third was to help bring us rain and sun during the proper seasons.

Since the skies were still somber, I prayed for sun, hoping that with the sun's return everything would suddenly brighten, including the state of Matunherí's health.

HALF MOON, DAY 6

I had a puzzling dream that the sea rose to meet the land, covering all of Xaraguá. I woke up trembling and could not fall asleep again for trying to interpret this dream. I have these very terrible interpretations in mind: Does my dream mean that Matunherí is dying and that Xaraguá will soon be washed in tears? Is my dream the heavens' way of signaling that the sun will never surface again? Could it be that we should soon expect a defeating attack from the Kalinas? Perhaps they have heard about Matunherí's illness and are planning to attack us before he is better.

HALF MOON, DAY 7

Matunherí seems to be improving. He was able to eat a full meal at sunrise. I would like to be hopeful, but he has shown some improvements before, only to fall ill again.

The skies remain gray, with dusky clouds suspended over us in the most menacing way. All across Xaraguá, our corn is being harvested in a great hurry. Should these dark clouds remain, it will be some time before we are able to plant again.

HALF MOON, DAY 8

My uncle's health continues to vacillate; he decided to undergo yet another healing rite. One of his healers fashioned him a special vomiting stick so that he could purge himself in a more forceful manner, then Matunherí inhaled some potent tobacco, which induced a trance. While in the trance, he was better able to communicate with the spirits, who told him that a hurricane was coming. Now it is clear to me what my dream meant. According to Matunherí, we have little time to prepare.

Matunherí remains in a trance, even though he has not made any more declarations about the hurricane or anything else. Behechio and I called the subchiefs together quickly and asked everyone to prepare the best they could for the hurricane.

Bibi and Baba left their own house to join us at Matunherí's house. The servants collected food and water. They also gummed more palm and thatch to the roof and reinforced the wall around the courtyard. The subchiefs have made my uncle's visions known to all the villagers under their control. Hopefully all of our villages are now prepared for the hurricane.

A riddle involving hurricanes:

What is the difference between a war and a hurricane?

Response:

*A war we may be able to win with our own might, but
    with a hurricane, all power is out of our hands.*

HALF MOON, DAY 10

Still no hurricane, though the skies remain covered with dark clouds. Now and then we have a drizzle that we are sure is the beginning, but nothing has happened yet.

My uncle has resurfaced from his trance. If his eyes

had not moved now and then, we would have thought he was dead. The first thing he said when he rejoined us was, "Do not despair at a little rain. A drop of rain is the heavens' way of giving us an embrace."

We are still waiting to find out how brutally the heavens will embrace us.

FULL MOON, DAY 11

Though the skies have not cleared, my uncle's health seems to be getting better. He is eating regularly again and is able to walk in the courtyard with Behechio and me at his side.

He must have known that it was not his time yet, otherwise before he went into his trance of many moons he would have named either Behechio or myself — or both of us — as his successors.

FULL MOON, DAY 12

The sun came out again, but not for long. Matunherí took the opportunity to go for a sea bath. During our walk toward the sea, he told Behechio and me that when he first became ill, he thought it was because he had done something to displease our ancestors. But he's since realized that his long illness, which has not altogether disappeared, as he still coughs a great deal and quite often, may simply have been due to the fact that he is getting old.

FULL MOON, DAY 13

The sun is out. No hurricane yet. I am puzzled about Matunherí's declaration and my dream. If the hurricane does not come, will the people still trust my uncle's interpretations of the skies? And can I still trust what I see in my dreams?

Behechio said Matunherí is planning to call the sub-chiefs together to tell them that he pleaded with the heavens to spare us from the hurricane.

I am always with Matunherí when Behechio is with him, still they manage to have talks that I am not part of. I did not express this to Behechio, but I don't like having such important matters communicated to Behechio when I'm not present.

FULL MOON, DAY 14

From sunrise to sunset, no rain, just sunshine. Matunherí ordered a corn feast to celebrate the harvest and our being spared from the hurricane. All we ate was corn. Much of it was picked while still tender, so we ate the kernels raw. Older kernels were roasted or boiled or mashed into a powder. More corn was soaked in water and made into corn bread. We sang our elders' ballads about corn and told our elders' stories of past harvests that were nearly destroyed by rains but spared in the end.

Many of our villagers came to the feast to wish my uncle well. Yeybona and Piragua came, too, with their son. Nahe has grown so much and he is already walking. Yeybona tells me he is also a wonderful swimmer. With my uncle's illness and all my extra duties, I have not seen Yeybona, Piragua, and Nahe in some time. I hope to soon go fishing with Piragua, and swimming with Yeybona and Nahe. But first my uncle must get well.

FULL MOON, DAY 15

Behechio's way of celebrating the saved corn harvest is to choose three more women who he will eventually make his wives. (Matunherí now allows him to choose his own wives since Yaruba died.) Soon he will have seven wives, almost as many as my uncle. For a long time, he had not wanted to change the number since Yaruba died.

Baba and Bibi have gone back to working with the

servant carvers on the mortars and pestles trade. Bibi and I made some necklaces and bracelets with which to greet Behechio's new wives when they arrive.

LAST QUARTER MOON, DAY 16

We had a storm last night, a sudden and quick one.

The rain fell like large rock pellets and the winds were so powerful that they uprooted all the trees in my uncle's courtyard and blew away all the surrounding houses. I was so frightened, I could barely breathe. There is nothing more terrible than a disaster you can do nothing about, no matter how powerful or clever you are. On the contrary, all these things seem to work against you as you become motionless and helpless, the prey of nature's angry gods.

During the storm, we all gathered in Matunherí's house — the strongest house in Xaraguá. Matunherí's wives, Behechio and his wives, Bibi and Baba, and all the servants whose houses had already been destroyed by the winds were grateful to be under my uncle's protection.

The house swayed back and forth, so much that we thought it was going to be lifted off the ground. Fortunately, it withstood the rains, even though the winds blew away several layers of the thatch roof, resulting in water dripping in. Then, just as suddenly as it began, the storm stopped, or moved on, as Matunherí said, to somewhere else.

It was still dark when the winds and the rain died down, so none of us ventured outside to examine the damage, but I knew, as all of us knew, that the destruction was vast.

LAST QUARTER MOON, DAY 17

As soon as the sun came up, Behechio and I accompanied Matunherí to the villages to inspect the ravages of the storm. The ground was still muddy and soaked and many of the fields were buried under overflowing rivers. As we had suspected, many trees had fallen and several houses had been blown away. We don't know yet how many of our people have died, but a small group has already gathered around Matunherí's house to ask if their loved ones have been seen, alive or dead.

LAST QUARTER MOON, DAY 18

The dead are too many to count. The villagers continue to gather the bodies in the plaza facing the prayer house. A mountain of corpses is slowly forming: men, women, and children, servants, planters, growers, healers, fishermen, fighters, mothers, fathers, sons, daughters.

The higher ranking among the dead will be buried in caves. The other bodies will have to be burned, Matunherí says, to prevent the spread of illness. The ground is too soaked for us to bury them and the type of burial ground needed for so many would be much too difficult to dig now. Besides, there is no time for ceremony. The sky is overcast again, indicating more rain might come.

This is one of those moments that I do not envy Matunherí's position. I don't know how he keeps himself from crying. I myself cannot stop crying. In the pile are many people I know. Some are childhood playmates. Others have trained with us to defend ourselves from the Kalinas. How could the heavens have claimed them in this harsh and painful way?

Matunherí's weaver, Cuybio, brought us the worst news yet. Yeybona and Piragua and their son, Nahe, have perished. Their bodies were found in the remnants of their house.

Cuybio did not bring them to the courtyard, fearing they would be burned with the others. Instead he had already taken them to the sea and put them to rest there, beneath the waves.

I say this, among many other prayers, under my breath: *Yeybona and Piragua, who had so loved the sea, Nahe, who had been named for things of the sea, may your spirits be elated there. Attabeira, goddess of our rivers and all our waterways, these beings, so loved, have been placed in your bosom. Please offer them more favor than had been granted to them here, in the life they have just left.*

LAST QUARTER MOON, DAY 19

> *Bodies burn at dawn,*
> *Tower of flesh,*
> *Blinding smoke*
> *Blending with clouds.*
> *We, the people of the ground,*
> *And you, the people of the sky,*
> *Are even more allied now*
> *By this thread of smoke*
> *Arriving your way.*
> *We send them now,*
> *These pillars of our lives,*
> *To join with you*
> *Not as sacrifices*
> *For our transgressions*
> *Nor as spare souls*

For which we lacked space,
But we send them to you
Because you have already claimed them
With your windy embrace.
Look after them,
And look after them well,
For we will miss them
Long after this heap of flesh
Turns to ashes,
Long after this smoke
Vanishes into air.
We will remember them,
But we will also remember
That they are with you,
And each time you send us an embrace,
Tender or fierce,
We will remember
That they are embracing us, too.

LAST QUARTER MOON, DAY 20

The servants have cleared the remnants of the funeral pyre. It seems we have seen the last of the dead. The seas are calm. The sun has returned.

Matunherí is still ill, spending his days lying in his

hammock with his healers around him. Behechio, Bibi, Baba, and I, Matunherí's wives, and many of the subchiefs sit all morning outside his house, waiting for his fate to be decided by forces beyond ourselves.

We were on this solemn watch and I was remembering our recent dead when I looked up at the patch of blue sky immediately above our heads and saw that it was covered with birds. They were large, majestic birds, coated in feathers with more colors than the rainbow itself. These birds seemed to be forming a design. A circle, two circles? I was not sure.

And then I stood up to have a closer look and I recognized the birds. They were the same type of bird that Chief Caonabó had given me after my haircutting ceremony, the ones I had released from the cage and let fly away.

Now Behechio, Bibi, Baba, and Matunherí's wives were also looking up at the sky, admiring the birds.

"They are a good omen," Guamayto, Matunherí's first and favorite wife, said.

"We should tell the servants to bring them down with bows and arrows," Behechio said. "We need their meat."

"They look spectacular against the indigo sky," Bibi said, "like a colorful blanket."

"They are Chief Caonabó's birds," Baba said. These birds are only to be found in Maguana. Chief Caonabó

69

originated the species by breeding different types of birds so he could have singular feathers for his headdress.

"Why would Chief Caonabó have sent his birds to cloak our skies like that?" Baba asked. He was looking at me, smiling. So were Bibi and Behechio.

"What an extravagant man!" Behechio said, as if annoyed by such an immoderate display.

"This is how he announces his visits," Baba said. "This means that he will soon be coming to see us."

"We will need him," I said, trying to pace my speech so that it would not betray how exhilarated I felt. "He can help us with provisions until the next harvest."

"If he is allied with us in any way," Behechio said, as though he were already the supreme chief of Xaraguá, "then we will have the two most powerful regions in Quisqueya. Let him come, though we will not receive him as beggars but as equals."

At that moment, I realized it was Behechio and not I who would rule Xaraguá. In my mind, I surrendered sole authority to him, just as I would something I was holding in the palm of my hand. Xaraguá was now Behechio's to rule, not mine. And I was glad it was I who had made that decision, not him nor Matunherí. My future was with these birds.

THE SUNNY SEASON
FIRST QUARTER MOON, DAY 1

I call this the sunny season. It is my own special season, the period after a storm when everything begins to mend itself under the sun's watchful glow. It is a time when the ground smells fresh and new, as though it had been washed and scrubbed by the rains. It is a moment when the overturned soil is slowly beginning to find roots once again. It is a season when the sun remains out from dawn to dusk, and only disappears at the very final moment, when it is to be replaced by the moon.

Chief Caonabó's birds have disappeared from the skies, yet still he has not come. Behechio and I told Matunherí about the birds, but he showed no emotion as he lay in his hammock, staring up at his thatch roof. I couldn't help but fantasize that Matunherí was trying to look beyond the thatch, perhaps to envision the birds. I wish so much he had seen them.

FIRST QUARTER MOON, DAY 2

Behechio and I again brought up the matter of Chief Caonabó's possible visit with my uncle. Matunherí replied that as far as he was concerned, Chief Caonabó had not officially announced his visit because he hadn't sent proper messengers to ask if we would receive him. The birds were merely a diversion, a strange sort of amusement, Matunherí said. If Chief Caonabó did not announce his arrival in the usual fashion, he would not be received in the usual fashion, either.

In spite of what he said about not receiving Chief Caonabó well, Matunherí ordered that the plaza be cleaned and the houses that had been destroyed by the storm be rebuilt. The fallen trees were cleared out and now the village looks no worse for having suffered through the storm.

It seems Matunherí has decided that Chief Caonabó should not see him ill. He has made a special effort to get out of his hammock and stroll around the courtyard with help from his wives, especially Guamayto, who is always at his side.

First Quarter Moon, Day 3

Chief Caonabó's messengers have arrived. They announced that Chief Caonabó was set to leave Maguana soon after they did and we should expect him.

Matunherí was not too pleased that Chief Caonabó was already on his way. He would have liked to have given the messengers word of his approval for the visit to carry back to Maguana.

FIRST QUARTER MOON, DAY 4

We are still waiting for Chief Caonabó. Even though everyone appears to be aware of the purpose of his visit, I am doing my best to act as though his coming to Xaraguá is no concern of mine.

I go about all my activities as usual and when I want to go to the beach to watch for his ship, I pretend that I am going to the bluff to sit at the mouth of Yaruba's cave.

I hope Yaruba will forgive me this ruse. Somehow I think she would. It is beneath my stature to act in this manner. My grandmother would have never acted this way. But I am very anxious and cannot help myself.

A riddle with a painful answer:

> *What if Chief Caonabó's visit*
> *does not concern me at all?*

FIRST QUARTER MOON, DAY 5

Matunherí's health is showing some improvement again. It seems now that this is how he is meant to live the rest of his days, swinging unpredictably between sickness and health.

Maybe Chief Caonabó has changed his mind and is not coming after all. His messengers are still here, waiting for him to arrive. Because the messengers are here with us, observing everything, which they might later report to Chief Caonabó, Matunherí makes a special effort to go about his duties, as if he were well. Still, the sight of these men irritates him. What's more, Chief Caonabó's messengers eat a lot. But we must continue to show them the same courtesy as we would Chief Caonabó himself.

I do my best to avoid Chief Caonabó's men. I often catch them staring at me during the communal meals and following me during my afternoon walks. Often they rush ahead to cut a tree limb with an ax or uproot a dense bush in my path or shoot arrows at tree rats or birds dangling on high branches above my head. I have asked them to stop doing this, but it's no use. They continue.

HALF MOON, DAY 6

Behechio and I met with Matunherí, at his request, after the communal meal at dusk. Behechio said that if Chief Caonabó does not come soon, he will send his messengers back to Maguana. They are eating too much of our food and they loaf all day, unless they are watching me.

I have had many dreams now of Chief Caonabó's ship capsizing at sea, resulting in his death. Could it be that my fears and anxieties are creeping into my dreams? How can I be sure that this very tragic event has not already taken place?

I went for a long walk on the beach, watching the horizon for distant storms. The skies seemed clear, but it's hard to be certain in matters concerning the sea. Something could have happened to Chief Caonabó's ship, somewhere in the waters between here and Maguana.

I noticed Chief Caonabó's men watching me. I walked up to them and before I could speak they said, "Please forgive us, but we are only following the wishes of our chief."

"And what is the wish of your chief?" I asked.

"To be sure no ill comes to you," they said.

I thought this very insolent of their chief. Haven't I lived my whole life without his protection? What made him think I would need it now?

I was so aggravated, I almost forgot what I had walked up to say to them. It wasn't to scold them. It was simply to ask if they were not fearful for their chief.

They were not worried, they said. If something had happened to Chief Caonabó, he would have sent them a signal.

"What kind of signal?" I asked.

Birds, they said. Black birds of peril, which he always traveled with for this purpose.

Birds! Of course! I should have known.

If the chief were in peril, they said, the skies would be covered with black birds.

Again, the skies were as clear as on any beautiful day. There were no signs of black birds anywhere. Still, considering Chief Caonabó's extreme fascination with birds, I am beginning to think he is short a few feathers himself.

HALF MOON, DAY 7

Chief Caonabó has appeared. At last! I am surprised at the joyous feelings his arrival has stirred in me. I did not see him for very long, but only caught a peek as he was entering Matunherí's house with his men. From what I could see, he appeared spent from his journey. Before Chief Caonabó could see me, Bibi quickly took me away from Matunherí's yard, for reasons she did not need to explain. In my absence, it seems, I might be a more valuable conquest than in my unmasked presence.

Half Moon, Day 8

I am once again with Baba and Bibi, with orders from my uncle not to appear at his house until he sends for me. Oh, what games! According to Baba, Chief Caonabó slept soundly after his long journey, which was quite difficult. He encountered rough seas, and nearly lost his life. Still he did not release the black birds of peril. How brave!

Half Moon, Day 9

I thought Matunherí had forgotten me, but finally he sent for me. Bibi and Baba came along with me to his house before the sunrise meal. When we arrived, Behechio was already there, along with many of the subchiefs from the villages and Chief Caonabó with a small group of his counselors.

Bibi had seen to it that I was wearing my most beautiful coral-and-gold ear and leg ornaments, but none of them matched the splendor of Chief Caonabó's bright, feathered headdress and shiny belt and breastplate. I did my best to avoid looking at him and to appear indifferent, as Bibi had advised, but it was quite difficult as my uncle spoke at length.

He felt his health was not improving, Matunherí said. He knew that he was soon to join the ancestors. He did not want to leave Xaraguá weakened, so he was proposing an alliance between Xaraguá and Maguana, which would make both territories stronger and more resilient to the Kalinas and even to natural hazards like windstorms and hurricanes.

"Chief Caonabó has asked to marry our treasured Anacaona," he continued. "And we have accepted. But since it is also Anacaona's fate to rule Xaraguá along with Behechio, she must accept Chief Caonabó's offer herself."

Suddenly, I felt every eye on me. It was as though I was holding the fate of Xaraguá in my hands. At the same time, I was glad that my choice was so plain, so simple. Before me was someone I already admired and might even love. I could have had this same offer from someone I despised. Rather than marry someone I hated, I would have remained in Xaraguá. But with the great opportunity that this marriage presented — how could I refuse?

I could hear Matunherí's laborious breathing filling up the whole room. More than anyone else, even more than Chief Caonabó perhaps, Matunherí was eagerly waiting for my reply. It was as if he had been postponing his last breath for this, some hope that he could craft a better future for Xaraguá.

Matunherí's difficult breathing made me feel terribly sad. It seemed certain that he would leave us soon. If he were to die, I wanted him to leave us with no worries about Xaraguá's future, a future that depended partly on my decision. I had never felt so much like a *cacica*, more like a mature person, more like a woman, in my entire life. I had never felt more like my grandmother, who I was certain would have made the exact same decision had she been in my position. And though neither Xaraguá nor Matunherí was the sole reason I chose to link my fate to Chief Caonabó's, they were both why I hastened to say those words so quickly, "Anacaona accepts."

Yes, I accept. It seems as if there could have been no other choice. Even Chief Caonabó must have known that this was the only thing I could say. And in spite of Bibi's warnings for me to appear calm, I appeared more delighted than perhaps I should have in accepting Chief Caonabó. I raised my head and stood up straight and looked Chief Caonabó directly in the eye. I did not shuffle my feet or slump and I certainly did not whisper as though I was merely making a concession, a sacrifice for my people, as though I was simply giving in. For indeed I was not giving in. I was giving myself. And I was doing so freely and gladly. I was saying yes with my whole heart.

Though it was obligatory and important, I felt that we would no longer need a marriage ceremony. In my mind a pact between myself and Chief Caonabó had already been sealed. I had bound myself to him and in the process had coupled Xaraguá and all our powers and riches with Maguana.

HALF MOON, DAY 10

Preparations have already begun for my marriage. Word has gone out all through the territories of Quisqueya that I am to be Caonabó's wife. Caonabó has already returned to Maguana to arrange his bridal offering and to put into position a home for me there. Before his departure, Matunherí read the stars and decided that Caonabó and I should marry at the final appearance of the last quarter moon.

I wish I'd had some time alone with Caonabó before he left, but Matunherí would not allow us to see each other outside the official meetings. We are to remain apart until we marry. This is how it has been with all of Behechio's wives. They were all strangers to him. I do not want to marry a stranger. I would rather marry an ally, a friend, but the honor of Xaraguá is linked to my actions so I must do exactly as my uncle says.

Our customs dictate that I am to remain in isolation in a special chamber of Matunherí's temple until the day of my marriage. I will have no hand in the marriage preparations, I will do nothing at all, except reflect and pray to the heavens and plead my ancestors' favors for the courage and grace to be a good wife. Every choice, from what to wear on my body to the dances that will be performed at the feast, will be made by Matunherí. At least Bibi, who knows my tastes and preferences, will be there to assist him. Food will be brought to me in the temple by servants who have orders not to speak to me. I will be very lonely. However, this period of contemplation and solitude will prepare me to slowly release my old life and accept my new one.

FULL MOON, DAY 12

My final moments out in the world, with the living. For the next few moons, I will be alone with my thoughts.

Bibi and I went to the river for a bath with Matunherí's and Behechio's wives, who all had some counsel for me. *"Be obedient." "Do as Chief Caonabó says. He is the ruler of Maguana, not you." "Be kind to everyone." "Learn to love your new land." "Don't do like Yaruba."*

Guamayto had the best advice of all: "Love him so much that if he should die, you would readily be buried with him, but if he should live, you would be even more joyful." This gave us all pause, as we knew that Matunherí did not have much time left and it seemed as if Guamayto was telling us that she was ready to follow the custom and be buried with him at the time of his death.

At the morning meal, Matunherí did not seem very well, sitting upright only with the help of a new, specially crafted chair that allowed for the weakness in his back. He had difficulty speaking, and I wondered if I would have to be called from the temple to attend his burial before my marriage. No one looked upon him with too much sadness, though, the way we might have at any other meal where he seemed so frail. Everyone was much too joyous at the prospect of my marriage, the happiness of one event balancing the sadness of the other.

Behechio was more attentive to me, seeing to it that I had as much to eat as I wanted, passing the communal plate in my direction, moving it away from Matunherí, who did not have much of an appetite.

Since Matunherí could barely speak, not many words were said at the morning gathering, and it was with this same silence, with the weight of both joy and pain upon us, that Bibi and Baba and Matunherí and Behechio escorted me to the temple chamber door and bid me a solemn farewell.

Before they left, I asked to have a few final moments with Cuybio's creation, upon which I have been recording these past seasons of my life. A servant will soon come to take these from me. It is to be given to Bibi for safekeeping, until I depart for my new life in Maguana, and begin to save my thoughts again.

LAST QUARTER MOON, DAY 20

During the interminable sunrises and sunsets of my isolation period, I not only rested and slept but also prayed to the ancestors, especially to my grandmother, for the courage to leave Xaraguá. Finally, I woke up one morning to find Matunherí standing over me in the temple.

"The time has arrived," he announced.

He seemed happier and stronger than he had appeared in some time and this gave me hope that everything was going to be well, not only for me but for him, too. He had a small cauldron in his hand filled with a warm drink; he asked me to drink all of it and I did. As soon as the warm, bitter liquid passed my lips, I felt my head growing lighter, my skin tingling, and I realized I was slowly falling into a trance, a mild one, where I was slightly numb but could vaguely follow what was going on around me.

Matunherí then left and Bibi and all the wives came in soon after. Bibi appeared calm. She seemed very pleased and happy with me. With help from Matunherí's wives, she raised me to my feet and carried me to the river to bathe me.

The path we took to the river was a new one, covered with smooth and freshly polished stones. It had been made especially for me on the day of my marriage. After my bath, where I was scrubbed with all types of cleansing and fortune-bearing herbs, I was taken back to Bibi's house and my body was painted. Bibi placed some gold ornaments on my legs and neck and tied a flower-scented band of cloth around my arm to symbolize the binding nature of marriage. Then Baba appeared and took me to a small house near the plaza, a place that had been built especially for my temptation ceremony.

It was an open room and in the middle was a chair Baba had carved for me out of wood, stone, and manatee bone. He led me to it and I sat down. I knew this temptation ritual well, having hidden in the woods to watch it each time Matunherí performed a marriage ceremony.

Fifteen of the strongest and most handsome men from

Xaraguá came into the temptation house and spoke to me of their virtues. Some told me they were rich. Others asked me to look at how handsome they were, and consider how patient they were, how kind. Many asked if I was certain I wanted to marry Caonabó and not them. By then Baba had disappeared, leaving me alone with the men who had been carefully picked by Matunherí for this special purpose.

I refused them all and, after the last one had departed, walked out of the house, which was separated from the plaza by a wall of palms, and shouted in my loudest voice "*Maricato!*" That meant I had not only proven myself strong enough to resist a final temptation but had chosen the really strong one, my Caonabó.

My shout was heard in the plaza and a roaring cheer came back in response, as all assembled were made aware that I was going to honor my decision to marry Caonabó.

I was feeling much more myself, even though still light-headed from Matunherí's potion. The potion was meant to make me weak so I would make my choice of marrying Caonabó with both a clear and a cloudy head.

After the temptation ceremony, Bibi and Matunherí's wives returned to the new house along with Behechio's wives. The wives formed a line by their order of marriage — Guamayto led the procession and Behechio's most recent wife, his tenth, ended it. Baba had crafted a special marriage stool for me. It was covered with gold and seashells, which glistened in the sun. The servants carefully raised me up on the stool and carried me out to the plaza on their heads.

The plaza was teeming with people, even more than had been present for my hair ceremony. There were special places reserved for important visitors, chiefs and subchiefs from all over Quisqueya, all wearing their most beautiful belts and headdresses, all with their faces and bodies painted.

For a brief moment as I was carried to the marriage altar where Caonabó and Matunherí were sitting in their own elaborately decorated chairs, I looked over at the rows and rows of special guests and saw Caonabó's brother, Manicaotex, a subchief of the Maguá territory, whom I mistook for Caonabó. They looked so much alike that I thought Manicaotex was Caonabó and the man sitting at the altar next to Matunherí was someone else. However, the closer I got to Caonabó, the more like himself he looked.

As my stool was lowered to the ground, Caonabó waited for Matunherí to stand up to welcome me, then he did, too. Caonabó was holding a golden scepter almost as tall as he was. His teeth were filed thin and painted black and decorated with lavish stones and shells. His body was covered with ornamental symbols from Maguana. There were drawings of birds and serpents, rivers and hills, all neatly sketched on different parts of him. His flesh told the story of and paid homage to his land, its beauties and abundance, which would later be sung by one of his musicians at the marriage feast.

Caonabó got up and walked over to meet me. He presented an elaborate necklace of feather, bone, and coral, one of his many bridal offerings, to Baba and Bibi before they backed away from the altar. Matunherí then lit one of his pipes and blew the tobacco smoke to the four corners of the wind. There was the beating of the ceremonial drums, performed by Behechio, then Matunherí said the marriage blessing. Manicaotex offered the golden scepter Caonabó had held in his hand to Matunherí. And with that we were married.

The celebration lasted the duration of the new moon, during which the history of both Maguana and Xaraguá were sung, accompanied by maracas, drums, and stringed instruments. Matunherí organized pilgrimages to the hills and mountains of Xaraguá, where offerings of foods and animals were made to our first ancestors and to Yúcahu, god of the yucca, and Attabeira, goddess of our rivers and waterways and of fertility. There were many dances to Yúcahu and Attabeira and even one to me, performed by a group of young girls from the villages. They called it the Areito Anacaona. A group of young men performed an Areito Caonabó as well.

Through the whole celebration, Caonabó sat with my uncle and the other chiefs, smoking tobacco and drinking potions like the one Matunherí had given me the morning of my marriage. I sat with Matunherí's and Behechio's wives, who repeated the same advice they had given me at the time of my river bath. During the feast, the servants loaded Caonabó's ship with my belongings. At sunrise, I said good-bye to Baba, Bibi, Behechio, and Matunherí, kissing their hands and feet respectfully. Most of the people of Xaraguá had gathered on the beach to say good-bye to me, their Anacaona, their almost-ruler, their near-cacica. Wearing my new marriage skirt, which Bibi had made for me, I boarded the ship with Caonabó and slowly the seas carried me away from my beloved Xaraguá toward Caonabó's Maguana.

MAGUANA

1491

MY FIRST MAGUANA SEASON
FIRST QUARTER MOON, DAY 1

Maguana is beautiful. Just as I remember from my childhood visits, it is full of green hills and fertile valleys
joined by rivers whose beds glitter with gold. Its waters are
filled with more fish, turtles, iguanas, and manatee, than I
have ever seen in Xaraguá. As the ship approached her
harbor, I could see an abundance of canyons, gullies, caves,
and grottoes. It would take my entire lifetime to name
them all.

Rain trickled down on us upon our arrival day even
while the sun was shining. This resulted in the most beautiful rainbows. Maguana's people believe that rainbows
are large, colorful snakes that have risen up to the heavens
to drink from the clouds and that if you point at them,
they will reach down and bite your fingers. (I was tempted
to point at a very thick and beautiful rainbow to see what
would happen, but Caonabó sensed this and warned me
not to.)

On the beach where we landed, close to Niti, Caonabó's village, the sand is fine and white and there are some magnificent rocks that appear to have been molded by the most skilled carvers in all of Quisqueya, even though they were actually fashioned by the movements of the sea.

Caonabó's house is a most extravagant settlement, with all the other houses in the village built in a circle around his. (I should say *our* house, as it is now my house, too.)

Our house faces the plaza, where feasts and ball games are held under every phase of the moon. And our doors and windows are constructed in such a way that we do not even have to leave our hammocks to view the plaza and the events taking place there.

During a ceremonial *batey*, a ball game that was organized to welcome me to Maguana, the leader of the game, the son of a subchief, was so ashamed to have lost that he pierced his chest with a poisoned arrow and died. I was horrified by this strange welcome and immediately asked Caonabó to command that no one kill himself for losing a ball game in our presence — after all, if we did such things in Xaraguá, Behechio would be long dead — but Caonabó told me that it was important that honor be taught as well as shown and the man who killed himself was showing honor. (Maybe this is where Yaruba learned this type of honor.)

Everything happens quickly in Maguana, and the poor man's corpse was soon removed from the field. The celebration continued, but we left the ball game because Caonabó wanted to show me some of the wonders of his land before dark.

FIRST QUARTER MOON, DAY 4

As Caonabó and I are traveling, visiting many small villages in Maguana, I have been taking note of all the exceptional fruits that can be found here. We have many of them in Xaraguá, too, but they appear much larger here.

During our walks through Maguana's villages, I have seen peppers the color of blood, annattos that could be mistaken for hibiscus, cotton-fruit soursop with seeds as large as cocoa pods, and pineapples larger than my head. Wherever we stop to rest, we are offered many gifts: hammocks, canoes, and birds, which Caonabó adores. In one day, we have collected so much more than we could ever use. Thus whatever we are given in one village, we distribute in the next. All except the birds, of course, which Caonabó has ordered the servants to look after with all their vigilance.

Caonabó says that these gifts are really mine. The

people offer them to me to make me feel welcomed. But I don't need gifts to feel welcomed. The warm manner in which people have treated us already shows that they are happy to see me. I do my best to show them that I, too, am happy to see them, that I'm overjoyed to be in their land, at the side of their ruler.

As the people line up on the side of the road to greet me, they call my name together with Caonabó's, shouting "Anacaonabó!"

When I was a girl and dreaming of taking my place at the head of my people, I had always imagined that my name would be joined with that of my brother, Behechio, he who was meant to rule with me. But the stars intended for me to become Anacaonabó. And so it is.

The people of Maguana even call out that Caonabó and I are their "warriors" because Caonabó has fought the Kalinas so many times. I am startled to hear myself called a warrior, for even though I have trained to defend my people, I have not yet had a chance to prove myself. But now, by the simple nature of our association, whatever Caonabó is, I am, too.

FIRST QUARTER MOON, DAY 5

A hunting day for Caonabó. We spent the night at the village of his good friend Bayahibe, a subchief he has known since childhood. Caonabó and Bayahibe left at dawn and returned at dusk with plenty of fish and meat for supper. Bayahibe's beautiful young wife, Simihena, took me to a magnificent waterfall, where we spent our day splashing in the mountain streams. We walked in and out of the surrounding caves, their walls covered with turquoise, amethyst, and jade stones. Simihena has a kind and gentle face and reminds me very much of Bibi as well as my dear friend Yeybona, who was killed in the hurricane.

FIRST QUARTER MOON, DAY 6

As we left today, Simihena gave me a beautiful lightning stone. The stone, which is as wide and flat as my palm, is completely smooth, except for the tiny hole in the middle where the lightning struck it. I am stunned that the lightning did not break the stone altogether when it hit it. Holding this stone in my hand reminds me that perhaps this almost transparent rock acquired its beauty during the same hurricane that took the lives of my friends. But nature, as Simihena tells me, is as marvelous a carver as she is a destroyer.

95

Simihena comes from a family of carvers. Her mother, like my father, used to make ceremonial masks and amulets for her village. After her mother's death, the task fell to Simihena. I invited her to come and see me anytime she liked. Aside from Caonabó, Simihena is my first friend in Maguana.

HALF MOON, DAY 7

Caonabó and I have returned to our house. I am tired, but very happy. To welcome us back, the servants planted bright golden flowers — in other words, anacaonas — in the garden. A flock of Caonabó's beautiful birds were also released. But fear not, they have been trained to return. Besides, we have so many now that soon Caonabó's birds will outnumber the villagers.

HALF MOON, DAY 8

Caonabó is once again performing his usual duties, overseeing the morning and evening meals, meeting with his subchiefs, and appointing planting, hunting, and fishing duties to the people in his village. Watching him carry out his role as chief, I feel as though I am watching my uncle as a younger man. I have had no unfavorable news of Matunherí, but no favorable word, either.

Though Caonabó's advisers and servants show much respect, no one shows friendliness toward me. It is as if friendliness, which I am in need of most, is beyond my stature.

From sunrise to sunset today, while Caonabó fished and hunted, I remained alone in my hammock, resting while staring at the thatch above my head. Not that I didn't know this before, but my suddenly empty days are reminding me that to be the wife of the cacique is not at all the same as being the cacica.

HALF MOON, DAY 10

While lying in my hammock, I suddenly craved the taste of a guava and asked one of the servants to bring me one from a tree. A pile of guavas as tall as myself was brought to the front of the house. This is what it is to be Caonabó's wife. Every one of my desires can be realized immediately.

Caonabó has been training with his warriors. He instructs them regularly to prepare for Kalina attacks. When he is not away training, hunting, or performing some other duty, Caonabó and I are always surrounded by so many people — his servants, my servants, the messengers, the merchants, the counselors, the subchiefs, the healers, of which he has several. I suppose this was also true in Matunherí's household, though I had grown accustomed to it and never noticed it at all.

I asked Caonabó if I could accompany him on a hunt and he said yes without hesitation. He was surprised by my skill with a spear, which I learned from my grandmother's old warriors. I could have killed many creatures, but only a small pheasant was sacrificed for my desire to show how accurately I can reach my aim. I am now also welcome to train with the warriors and I shall, as much as Caonabó does.

A few more women have joined me in the hunt with Caonabó and his group. They are some of the most important women in our village. Simihena has been too taken with her duties to come and see me. Though I could command that she come and keep me company, this is no way to make and keep a friend.

I now have my own hunting dog, a gift from Caonabó. It is a beautiful dog with fur the color of sand. It snarls, but does not bark, which makes it easier for it to approach and catch its prey. It is well trained, as it was bred for Caonabó himself. At times, I hunt alone for my own pleasure, but for only as much meat as we can use.

FULL MOON, DAY 13

Caonabó and I are talking more and more, and slowly the large groups around us are disappearing at dusk. I told Caonabó about my desire to work with Simihena and some of the other carvers in Maguana and he said I should take charge of all such work in Maguana. Touching my chin, he said, "Golden Flower, all of Maguana is yours. You must only be willing to have it."

FULL MOON, DAY 14

While Caonabó and Bayahibe were fishing, I finally gave in and sent for Simihena and she came. I cannot force her to be my friend; I simply needed to see her. I discovered something else that Simihena and I share. She loves to dance and with a large group of girls performs at feasts and ceremonies. I agreed to sing some ballads for her girls and she asked me to think of some new shapes for the carvers. We will be working together now. After she left, I stared at the ground for hours, waiting for some carving patterns to emerge like flowers out of the soil.

LAST QUARTER MOON, DAY 15

Last night I had a dream that involved the sun. This is the first time I have ever dreamt about the sun. In my dream the sun had a face with eyes and a mouth, which it used to speak to me. "Look upon the earth," it said, "everything is there."

I spent the day looking at the earth. What secrets have the ancestors hidden for me in the earth of Maguana?

LAST QUARTER MOON DAY 16

> *Fade, full moon,*
> *As Anacaona's new life glows.*
> *If there is joy to be found here,*
> *Let her find it.*
> *If there is pain,*
> *Let her endure it.*
> *If there is love,*
> *Give her all there is.*
> *And as the moon is made new*
> *So will she.*

Last Quarter Moon, Day 17

I wanted to sing my new ballad for Simihena, but I did not want her to think I am unhappy. There are moments when I feel great joy here, sitting at Caonabó's side at the meals or talking to Simihena and the other women, who are slowly getting accustomed to my presence. But at other times, I also miss Baba, Bibi, Behechio, and my uncle so much. It is as if there is a large, empty space in me, a dark star that neither sun can light, nor moon shade, nor Caonabó with his kindness and love blot out.

Last Quarter Moon, Day 19

I have new shapes for the carvers. I was staring at my shadow on the ground when it came to me. Why not carve ourselves? Simihena will carve Simihena. I will carve Anacaona. I will carve my memories of my ancestors. The Night Marchers. My grandmother. I will also carve the living people who are missing from my life: Bibi and Baba and my uncle and even Behechio. I will carve them with my own hands. I will carve them the way the lightning carved Simihena's stone. (For why shouldn't our work be as beautiful as nature's?) I will carve Caonabó's strong and handsome image. I will carve images of caves, of the way our world was created. And in addition to all that, I will make ceremonial chairs, effigy vessels, ceramic flasks, bowls, graters, scepters, baskets, headdresses, pendants, stone collars, all with images of frogs, fish, and birds carved into them. Nothing will be carved in Maguana that will not bear the mark of Anacaona's heart or hand.

SEASON OF THE PEANUT HARVEST
FIRST QUARTER MOON, DAY 1

The smell of roasting peanuts fills the air. I never thought I could find such beauty in something so small — the coarse, furrowed shell the same tint as pale gold. The fragile, reddish brown skin and the seed itself, bronzed by the dark soil. I feel as though this harvest is just for me, for I have eaten so many of these marvels in so many different ways: raw, roasted, ground into a paste that can almost keep the mouth from moving.

I grow fatter with each mouthful, but have continued my usual activities and have even added new tasks to my days. I now write a ballad with every passing moon and feel free to sing them not only when I am alone but also for my Caonabó and Simihena, and I sing them while I fish or hunt, or carve, spin cotton fibers into cloth, or make necklaces.

First Quarter Moon, Day 2

A messenger came from Xaraguá with accounts from Matunherí and Behechio. Matunherí is well, remarkably, and Behechio has as many wives now as I have fingers and toes. Baba and Bibi would like to visit Maguana. I have al-ready sent the messenger with one of our best ships for them.

Caonabó has been stirring in his sleep. It seems as if something is troubling him in his dreams that even he is not aware of. When he wakes up, I ask him what it is that he saw in the night, but he cannot remember.

I envy Caonabó his dreams. Mine come less and less often, though it is possible that, like him, I see things at night that vanish in the air at dawn.

First Quarter Moon, Day 3

Manicaotex, Caonabó's brother, from the Magua region, has come to visit. Since Caonabó's parents are long dead, the two are mother and father as well as brothers to each other. We had a feast for Manicaotex and I sang several of my ballads and danced for him. How I envy Manicaotex and Caonabó! They are so loving and so loyal to each other. Though the regions they occupy are separate, they are one.

First Quarter Moon, Day 4

Manicaotex and Caonabó had a mock battle in the plaza at dawn. When others are watching, they usually swing their sticks in a vigorous manner. But this time no one was there (they didn't even know that I was), and they were encouraging and instructing each other in such a way that it was truly moving to observe. Seeing the sun slowly rise above their heads as they continued to train each other in this manner, I wished Manicaotex were always with us so that I would always have a moment such as this to wake up to.

Half Moon, Day 5

Already, Manicaotex has left. Caonabó seemed so happy when he was here. He was like a child at play. They hunted and fished and fought mock battles, both alone and in front of others. They also spoke of the affairs of their territory, of better defenses against the Kalinas, and of trade relations and other matters.

Half Moon, Day 6

While carving with Simihena and the other women today, I raised my head to watch a cloud pass above us, a cloud that was blocking out the sun. When I lowered my head, I saw among the shadows in the ground two sets of footprints, one very large and the other very small. And it returned, this sensation I have sometimes that I am receiving a message from someplace far, farther than the reach of my feet, from the land of the *opia*.

I pointed at the ground and asked Simihena if she saw the footprints, but once the cloud had passed over and the sunshine returned, only the bright red buds of the annattos remained.

HALF MOON, DAY 7

My beloved uncle has died. The messenger has just arrived with word of his passing from the land of the living to the ancestral world. Caonabó and I are soon to leave for Xaraguá.

HALF MOON, DAY 8

I find it hard to sleep at sea on my painful journey back to Xaraguá. Maybe I'm not at all a person of the sea, as I once thought.

Caonabó rests peacefully, as though he were being cradled by the waves. His black birds of peril ruffle in their cages. The flapping of their enclosed wings makes me even sadder. I look up at the stars and I know there is an additional one in the heavens — Matunherí guiding us back to him for our last farewell. Still, I feel as though there is part of the sea in my belly, for my stomach churns as much as the waters themselves. Could it be my sadness for Matunherí? My dread at seeing the sadness in Bibi's and Baba's faces? My worry that once I reach Xaraguá I will not want to leave it again?

HALF MOON, DAY 9

We have arrived in Xaraguá. Behechio greeted us at the shore. Seeing him and meeting his newest wives, none of whom have yet produced an heir, I remember that I am here not only for Matunherí's farewell but to see Behechio named the new cacique of Xaraguá.

Bibi is inconsolable. Baba tried to comfort her as they guided Caonabó and me to the temple to greet my lifeless uncle. Next to Matunherí sat Guamayto, who was waiting to say good-bye to us before taking the potion that would allow her to join Matunherí forever. Without question, I would do the same for Caonabó, die and be buried with him if necessary, but I was still too pained to touch

Guamayto's hand, knowing that she would soon be limp, covered in vegetable fibers, and wrapped tightly within a hammock, like Matunherí.

"Be brave, Guamayto," I whispered, fighting back my tears.

"He would be so lost in the next life without me," she said calmly.

"He would be," I said. "Look after him well and make sure the road is clear for us when our time comes."

I could not bear to stay and watch Guamayto swallow the potion that would also take her from us. So I walked out until I heard Bibi shout, "Guamayto is with him now."

HALF MOON, DAY 10

Matunherí and Guamayto were buried behind the temple, with their heads facing the sea. We squeezed as many quartz beads as we could into their hands and placed the shell of a freshwater turtle between their legs. We filled their burial plots with their amulets, Matunherí's effigies, and ceremonial axes and chairs. Even the pipes he enjoyed so much were buried with him and Guamayto. We also placed water-filled gourds near their heads and buried them with plenty of cassava bread for their nourishment in the next life. Ballads were sung to honor Matunherí's rule at a feast in the plaza. At the same feast, Behechio was named supreme chief of Xaraguá.

The sadness of Matunherí's passing was too much to bear. During Behechio's feast, my eyelids grew heavy and my body felt limp and I lost consciousness. When I woke up, I was lying in Bibi's house with Caonabó and Behechio and Bayaci and two of Behechio's healers around me.

"I thought I had died like Matunherí and Guamayto," I said.

"Anacaona is not dead," Bayaci said. "She is with child."

FULL MOON, DAY 11

Anacaona is with child! The word was passed from mouth to mouth in the room and later outside in the plaza, at the feast. As with our ancestors' lives, in our lives, too, joy and sadness are often intertwined. As with my vision of the two sets of footsteps in the sand, both Matunherí's large feet and my little child's small ones are walking the same path, but in different directions.

108

Full Moon, Day 12

Caonabó is extremely happy about our child. The life that lies ahead has relieved some of my own sadness about Matunherí. Pondering the new life lessens some of the pain of leaving Xaraguá. I wish Behechio well, as I know Matunherí would want me to. The future in me wishes him well, too.

Full Moon, Day 13

Bibi and Baba are not returning with me to Maguana. They want to stay to help Behechio, to counsel him in his new role. I want to tell them that I need them just as much as Behechio does. All his life Behechio has been trained to rule Xaraguá. I, too, had been trained to rule Xaraguá, but I have no training on becoming a mother.

Full Moon, Day 14

Before we left Xaraguá, Behechio called for Caonabó to discuss their new relations as chiefs. Caonabó insisted that I be present as well. Behechio appeared quite sure of himself as he spoke.

"Xaraguá will not be weakened," he said, "she will be strengthened with my rule."

He spoke in such a forceful and persuasive manner that I couldn't help but be very proud of him.

"No matter who or what comes, we will stand by your side," Caonabó added. "Your enemies will be our enemies. We know how to fight and we will fight them."

This was just the type of assurance Behechio was looking for.

LAST QUARTER MOON, DAY 16

I am still unable to sleep at sea on the return journey to Maguana. But now I know why my belly churns. Caonabó does not sleep, either, but remains awake with me. We watch the stars together, looking for a wink from our little dwarf star who will soon join us here on the ground.

MY HIGUAMOTA SEASON
FIRST QUARTER MOON, DAY 1

The time is quickly approaching when my child will be born. Caonabó thinks it will be a boy. I believe it will be a girl. I have the judgment of the soothsayers on my side. They believe the same as I do. They say they can tell by the shape of my belly. It is round and high, like a full moon.

I no longer have the strength to do anything but rest.

First Quarter Moon, Day 2

I am too tired to record much anymore. I lie in my hammock and wait for "my daughter's" arrival, making promises to the heavens and the ancestors and the stars, promises of gifts and offerings, should all go well.

I feel as though everything about me has grown, not simply the size of my body and the length of my hair. My vision has become sharper. I can hear and smell things from great distances. All this, even as each step has become harder to take.

Half Moon, Day 6

Bibi and Baba have come to visit. They bring word of Behechio now having even more wives, no child, but, like me, one on its way. It will be especially wonderful to have Bibi present for the birth of my little one.

Half Moon, Day 9

Simihena is here, too. She and Bibi and Baba have become great friends. Baba has counseled Simihena on carvings much more than I have been able to of late.

Full Moon, Day 12

She has arrived, my little one, my wonder of wonders. Just as I thought, she is a girl. We have named her Higuamota, after Caonabó's mother.

Full Moon, Day 13

Our Higuamota entrances Caonabó. It is as though he had never seen a child before. I think of Nahe and I shiver at all that can threaten a little life. I nearly want to weep, watching Higuamota's face rest in Bibi's hands. Everything I do now will be to shield and guard her precious life.

Full Moon, Day 14

Caonabó ordered a feast for Higuamota. At the feast he announced her name to all the villagers. The name was received very well.

She rarely cries, my Higuamota. Even when Bibi and Baba left us and returned to Xaraguá, she kept quiet as she watched me sob suddenly after seeing their canoe sail away.

Though I have had less time and strength to record every moment of my joy as well as all the new ballads I plan to write and the new shapes for carvings that she has inspired in me, I will always remember this season as my Higuamota season. Each time a full moon comes, it will always remind me of the one under which she was born.

LAST QUARTER MOON, DAY 20

This morning, my sadness is renewed at the memory of Bibi and Baba returning to Xaraguá. But at least they have promised to come back often to see us and watch Higuamota grow. To look into Bibi and Baba's eyes and my daughter's at the same time has made me so happy. Soon after they left, a messenger brought us word. Behechio is a father. At last, he has a son, whom he has named Guarocuyá.

Maguana

1492

THE WINDY SEASON
FIRST QUARTER MOON, DAY 1

The leaves flitter above our heads like birds ready to take flight. When the wind blows through the trees, it sounds as if nature is taking turns whispering and shouting. The fields sway; the flowers rise and fall, confusing the bees that usually feed from their blossoms.

Of course, Higuamota loves all this. Caonabó and I take her to a field where she can see and feel the heart of it, as though it is happening not only around her but *to* her.

She does not understand it all yet — the force of the breeze as it swells into a gusty draft and the calm that follows once it flattens — yet she likes it. We can tell by her broad smile. She extends her little hands as though to touch what it is not possible to touch: the air moving back and forth; the shriek of her father's birds from high above the clouds. Caonabó and I are always so glad to see it: our little one announcing herself to the birds and the wind with one joyous laugh.

Chief Guacanagarí, cacique of the Marién region, has come to visit. He was not trying to reach Maguana, but his ship was thrown off course by the winds while he was on a trade journey to the Higüey region.

Of all the regions of Quisquera, Marién has been the most frequently attacked by the Kalinas. Chief Guacanagarí took advantage of being with us to ask what he should do.

For an older man, Chief Guacanagarí is quite pleasant to look at. He has a solid build, sturdy and robust, is long-limbed and supple. He knows many old ballads, and tells stories about dead caciques, droll tales that make us laugh. He also spent a lot of time playing with Higuamota, who he says he'd like to marry to one of his sons when she is older. Still, Caonabó reminds me that Chief Guacanagarí is desperate and deeply concerned about attacks upon himself and his people, and his friendliness should never be regarded as loyalty.

Chief Guacanagarí and Caonabó have been by the sea from sunrise to sunset speaking to the ancestors and to each other. Chief Guacanagarí is quite distressed about the situation with the Kalinas. They have raided his territory more times than it has rained there, he said.

Caonabó has offered to go to Chief Guacanagarí's region to help train his people to fight, an offer gladly accepted by Chief Guacanagarí. Caonabó will have to make good on this promise soon.

Whenever Caonabó goes to Chief Guacanagarí's territory, I will go with him. For the Marién is a region I have always wanted to know better. When we go, we will leave our Higuamota with Simihena, who is quite fond of her.

First Quarter Moon, Day 4

The seas are a bit calmer now, so Chief Guacanagarí has left. He reminded Caonabó of his promise to him before his departure, and Caonabó said that he'd soon send word to Chief Guacanagarí about coming to Marién.

After Chief Guacanagarí left, Caonabó once again began training with his own men, and Simihena, Higuamota, and I went to a special stream in the mountains, the warm waters of which are said to have all kinds of healing properties, especially for children.

Higuamota's body and mind grow a bit more every day. In the stream, she looked me right in the face and whispered "Bibi" for the first time. Oh, how I love her, my

Higuamota! I didn't think it was possible to love someone this way, with all one's heart and soul. It is the same way I love her father, the way — I fully understand now — that Bibi and Baba must love Behechio and me.

FIRST QUARTER MOON, DAY 5

I have finally learned the source of Caonabó's fascination with birds. One of his servants, an old Kalina woman named Marahay, who's been looking after Caonabó since the day he was born, explained it to me. By chance, I asked her if Caonabó had loved birds since he was a boy, and she said when he was young his mother had told him about our ancestor Mácocael who had been locked out of the cave from which we all originally came and had been transformed into stone. Then she told me a part of the story I hadn't known. After Mácocael had become stone, the sun transformed him into a nightingale. From the moment he'd heard that story, Caonabó decided that all birds were wonderful and perfect.

HALF MOON, DAY 6

I am intrigued by Marahay. She is a Kalina living among Taínos, yet she is not our enemy. Marahay's story is quite interesting. When she was a girl, she was captured by Caonabó's father during a raid on her village.

Usually it is Kalina men who capture Taíno women during raids, so most Kalina women and children speak our language and the Kalina men speak a separate language. However, Caonabó's father had wanted to show the Kalinas that Taíno men were as strong as they were. He and his men had attempted a raid on Marahay's village, but they had only come away with Marahay, then a young servant in the household of a village warlord. Unhappy where she was, Marahay had willingly surrendered to them. Thanks to Marahay, Caonabó has learned many of the Kalinas' ways, and it is because of her that he has been able to protect his people against them. Since she was raised in the household of a warlord, Marahay knows the Kalinas' warrior language, Galibi, which she taught Caonabó as he was growing up.

I asked Marahay to teach me a few Galibi words to use in a ballad. I have hated the Kalinas for so long that I would like the words to help soften my heart, even if just a little. I also asked her to explain some of the Kalinas' customs and she told me how the Kalinas saw in their rainbows a serpent god they named Joulouca. She described how before they raided our territories, the men would cover their bodies with animal fat and ashes so they couldn't be seen in the dark. They also strung the teeth and bones of their victims into necklaces, which they wore as a sign of their prowess.

Marahay cooked me some meat stewed in hot peppers and manioc juice, a dish the Kalinas call pepper pot. She weaved me one basket as wide as a headdress and another as large as a winnowing tray, both in the simple style of the Kalinas. When Caonabó returned from the hunt, he joked that Marahay was trying to make me into a Kalina woman, but he ate heartily from the savory pepper pot Marahay had prepared and cradled Higuamota in one of Marahay's baskets.

I want Higuamota to know all the Kalinas' ways, in case we still have the Kalinas to fear when she becomes a woman.

HALF MOON, DAY 7

Today while Marahay and the other servants looked after Higuamota, I went to war training with Caonabó. Since I am so interested in the Kalinas' method of warfare, Caonabó showed me how they burn chili peppers to blind their enemies with stinging smoke when they enter a village. I could barely keep myself from clawing my eyes as we ran through the peppered smoke with only our fingers to shield our faces. What's worse, we had to attempt our escape even as our fighters, acting as Kalinas, threw poisoned arrows at us. I am lucky to have survived the training. Or as Caonabó would say, I survived because I am well trained. The more I escape harm during these exercises, the better I want to be. For Maguana, for myself, for my daughter, I want to be a true warrior.

HALF MOON, DAY 8

Last night, I dreamt that Joulouca, the Kalinas' rainbow god, split into several bands and scattered into pieces on the ground. One of the pieces fell in my hammock and grew into a rope, slithered up my body, and wrapped itself around my neck. At first it only tickled my gullet, but then its grip grew tighter, until I could hardly breathe. I reached up to pull it from my neck, but felt nothing there but air.

I woke up gasping for breath. In the dark, I stumbled around, looking for Caonabó and Higuamota. Both were sleeping peacefully. When I stepped outside, there was no rainbow in the dark sky, just the moon and a few stars, preparing their escape before dawn. One of the stars suddenly plunged from the clouds, landing somewhere far away.

Half Moon, Day 9

I described my dream to Caonabó and he thinks that the things Marahay has been telling me are taking up too much space in my head. Perhaps he is right. I have never thought of rainbows as menacing before. Now I will never be able to look at one in the same way — and I certainly won't even think of pointing a finger at one now.

Half Moon, Day 10

I couldn't sleep last night. I was so worried the rainbow serpent would come and choke me that I couldn't close my eyes. I held Higuamota all night, rocking her in my hammock and singing ballads in her ears. She is such a peaceful creature. Was I ever as tranquil and gentle as she seems? Was there a time when my nights were free of all but pleasant meditations? I also thought of Behechio's son. I must plan a trip to see him, to hold him in my arms and rock him, too. I want Higuamota to meet him and love him, to play with him the way I played with Behechio when he was a boy.

Full Moon, Day 11

I carved a wooden rainbow with Simihena and the other women today. We painted it with vegetable dyes and left it out under a tree to dry. This painted rainbow serpent is my peace offering to the Kalinas' rainbow god, Joulouca. Maybe now he will befriend me and leave my dreams alone.

Full Moon, Day 12

Manicaotex sent a messenger with an odd word. Three ships filled with men with pale skins have landed on the shores of Marién, the region where Guacanagarí rules. Caonabó listened closely to the messenger, then began laughing. I myself found nothing to laugh at in this message. Disturbed by his great fear of the Kalinas, perhaps Chief Guacanagarí had heard the Night Marchers beating their drums and had seen the shadows of their dimmed torches on their slow march toward the sea, Caonabó said. But as Manicaotex's messenger told it, these creatures had walked out of and not into Chief Guacanagarí's seas.

Caonabó kept laughing as he listened to the messenger. I was not amused. Besides, if Chief Guacanagarí had seen the Night Marchers so clearly, wouldn't he be dead?

Caonabó sent Manicaotex's messenger away with word to his brother to tell Chief Guacanagarí to stop inhaling so much tobacco that he would mistake the phantoms induced by his trances for true beings.

FULL MOON, DAY 13

Things grow stranger still. Behechio sent a messenger with the same message as Manicaotex. Behechio's messenger, however, carried a few more details. Chief Guacanagarí has befriended these pale men, has fed and entertained them, offering them many gifts, as if they were esteemed visitors. These men, too, have offered Chief Guacanagarí gifts of small pieces of hide and metals and clear beads. Behechio's message signals that we must take these accounts seriously. Caonabó will leave for Marién soon and I plan to go with him.

FULL MOON, DAY 14

I have never seen Caonabó appear afraid before. My fearless warrior has been in the temple all day, speaking to the ancestors. These men, could they be kin to the Kalinas? Or are they a new type of warrior? They do not sound fierce like the Kalinas. Perhaps they are traders from distant lands. Do they have navels? Do they wish us well or are they here to harm us?

Full Moon, Day 15

The sea was too rough today, so we could not start for Marién. No other messengers have come, perhaps also because of the sea. I will leave Higuamota in the care of Simihena when we are able to travel. Knowing now that I will be with Caonabó on his journey, I join him in the temple and ask for guidance not only from his forebears but from mine, too, especially my grandmother who, during her time on Earth, had dreamt that men with skins as white as air would come to Quisqueya.

Last Quarter Moon, Day 16

The pale men have reached our shores. We were awakened at dawn by clamorous voices like none I have ever heard and the sight of men unlike any I have ever seen. They were tall, nearly twice our size. Their heads were as round as the full moon and what we could see of their skin — for they were covered in dark, heavy-looking materials from their shoulders down to their hide-clothed feet — was indeed pale, though not as pale as I had imagined.

Their hands and faces were slightly pink, as if only recently singed by the sun. Though they were in smaller numbers than us — I counted only four — they seemed to be in charge of our subchiefs, servants, and warriors, who had followed them from several villages inland and had fearfully led them to us.

As Caonabó and I emerged from our house, still rubbing the sleep out of our eyes, they immediately surrounded the plaza, each positioning himself in one of four corners, to point hollowed-looking metal sticks at us. From these sticks they fired bursts of lightning into the air, which startled and frightened our people, forcing many of them to flee.

Caonabó ordered our people to stand still. This did no good for the pale men kept firing their lightning rods at the clouds, frightening them even more. For a moment I thought I was dreaming. It was as if we were suddenly at war with gods. Only the piercing smell of smoke from these strange new weapons convinced me that I was awake.

Finally the pale men lowered their weapons and began moving closer to us. Their eyes were fair, the colors of jade and lapis, and many of our men were entranced by these colors and whispered to one another how these might be gods who had captured the sea in their eyes and could produce lightning at will. Standing now very close to us, the pale men spoke quickly in a tongue we of course did not understand. At times they turned and spoke to one another, then faced us once more, reaching over and stroking the gold ornaments around the necks, and arms, of our warriors. Pointing, they motioned to these ornaments and signaled for our men to surrender them. Without firing, the pale men aimed their lightning rods at those of our men who hesitated before turning over these decorative pieces of gold. To others they handed small chimes and pieces of metal, which our fighters accepted eagerly.

Now standing directly in front of me, one of the pale men reached over as if to rub my skin. Disgusted at his lack of respect for my superior stature, I pushed his dirty, fleshy fingers away. He reached for my arm a second time. Again I pushed his hand away. He laughed, but his bared teeth though unfiled and not pointed, looked so menacing that I removed my ear and nose ornaments and handed them to him. He abruptly raised them to his large, crowded teeth as if to chew them, then lowered them, looking pleased. I refused the small, transparent container he offered me in exchange for my ornaments, but a group of our fighters quickly traded their spears and body ornaments for it.

Caonabó stepped forward to the one who seemed to be the leader, for he stood slightly apart and appeared to be watching over the other three. His covering was also much more elaborate than the others' and on his head he wore a basketlike shield to protect his face from the early morning sun. As Caonabó approached him, he reached into his heavy clothes and produced some red beads on a string and pointed at Caonabó's golden leg ornaments. Caonabó quickly removed his ornaments and as a gesture of friendship accepted the modest-looking string for them.

"Where do you and your men come from?" Caonabó shouted in his face. Frankly I was even more perplexed now, for if these had been confused Night Marchers who had marched out of, rather than into the sea, wouldn't Caonabó shouting at them lead to all our deaths?

The pale man ignored Caonabó's question. Looking directly in my husband's eyes, he pointed at his own mouth and stomach as if to ask for food.

Caonabó immediately signaled to a group of servants to prepare food for our visitors. I could already see the strategy forming in Caonabó's mind. If these were angry spirits, perhaps we could appease them with a meal of yucca and pineapple. And with gifts of gold.

As the servants rushed off to prepare the food, Caonabó ordered our servants to bring four of his best chairs for our visitors. What was he going to do, my brave warrior? Did he perhaps believe that these were gods? Was he trying to soothe or spoil them?

Whoever they were, they were not familiar with our customs. For when the servants brought them Caonabó's most beautiful chairs, they did not receive this great honor by immediately sitting on the chairs, but walked around them and greedily tried to wrench pieces of gold from them with their bare hands. This is when our visitors' intentions became clear to me. They were neither spirits nor gods. They were not looking for courtesies, allies, or friends. They were only looking for gold.

I was so angered by the manner in which they were destructing our ceremonial chairs that I could no longer endure their presence. I turned around and went back into the house to see about Higuamota. She was cradled in Marahay's arms and looked up, wide-eyed and smiling, when I walked in. I told Marahay to take Higuamota inland to my friend Simihena, who I knew would look after her no matter what befell us next.

As Marahay was bundling up Higuamota, Caonabó

came in. He was assembling some of his golden chest plates to offer to our visitors. We did not have much time to talk, he said. But he had in mind a way to see if these pale men were like us or from some other world. He would convince one of them to go with him to the beach and force his head underwater. If he drowned, then he was human, but if he survived, he was a Night Marcher or some other form of apparition.

Whatever Caonabó wanted to do, I would consent to. But at this moment, what I wanted most was to move Higuamota as far from these men as I could.

As Marahay hurried from the house with Higuamota, running even faster once she spotted the pale men pulling apart our precious chairs, it was as if my heart had left my chest and was galloping from me. And I vowed to myself that there was nothing I wouldn't do to see my Higuamota again.

Suddenly, my heart did almost stop. One of the men fired his lightning stick at Marahay, who went stumbling forward with Higuamota. There was a cloud of smoke around Marahay and Higuamota as they both lay on the ground. Another of our servants rushed forward to collect my daughter. I myself was running to her, but the short distance seemed so far, until I reached her and took her from one of our warriors who had grabbed her off the ground, where she lay next to Marahay, who was still moaning there.

I was happy to have Higuamota in my arms again. She was unharmed, thankfully only a bit dusty. Marahay was not bruised or hurt. The firing stick had missed her, but had scared her so much that she had stumbled against a rock. All the agitation had frightened Higuamota so much that she was now crying. I, too, was crying, yelling in the direction of the man who had fired at Higuamota and Marahay. I can't remember all the words I shouted at him, for it seemed that from the time Marahay had fallen to the time I once again had Higuamota in my arms I didn't hear, see, or feel anything besides wanting to save her.

From across the plaza, Caonabó asked if Higuamota was hurt. He was so angry that his face was twisted and soaked with sweat. I replied that she was well and so was Marahay. As soon as he had my assurance that both Higuamota and Marahay were fine, Caonabó leaped at the man who had fired at them, letting out a thunderous cry, ordering his people to attack. As our warriors and servants all swooped down on the men, I ran inland, to see Higuamota safely to Simihena's house. Once Higuamota was safe, I would return, not only to avenge this one brutal act but to help assure that something like this would never happen again.

These four terrible men are dead. And I took part in it. I am trembling even now and find it very hard to elaborate on the extent of my participation. The way the villagers tell it, and I suspect the way the ballads will be sung and stories recited about this day, is that, soon after I fled with Higuamota, Caonabó's anger made him even bolder and braver than usual and he threw himself at the pale men's leader, wrenching the lightning stick from his hand while pounding a stone at his head until he was no longer breathing. Our warriors similarly attacked two of the others and, soon after, their bodies were taken to the sea and thrown into the waves so that if they had indeed fallen from the skies, they might immediately return to the skies from the sea. This is where I participated. Once Higuamota was safely with Simihena, I returned to our house to find one last pale man left in the plaza. He was bound with strong ropes to the chair that Caonabó had graciously offered him earlier, a beautiful *duho* he had tried to tear apart for gold.

This last man had not been killed because Caonabó was waiting for all his warriors to gather before he would take him to the sea to test whether he would survive under the waves. Somehow I knew (and I think Caonabó did, too) that this man would not survive the sea, especially if he was thrown in with his arms and legs bound. But I didn't stop Caonabó from gathering all the subchiefs and warriors to watch. Just as they had done with the others, our men removed his clothes to see if this last pale man had a navel. Watching, I could see that indeed he did have a navel, though it was small and ashen like the rest of his skin and was buried deep inside his large stomach. For a moment I had thought that perhaps these men were apparitions, entities that floated dangerously between the living and the dead, creatures that did have navels, but navels so small and white that you could barely see them.

When the last pale man was thrown, alive, into the sea, he sank like an empty vessel. Immediately, my heart sank, too. But my guilt did not last long. These creatures could have easily taken my daughter's life. And if they had, I would be the one disappearing now, beneath the waves, in their place. For surely my grief would be too much to bear.

Marahay is now resting. Our healer gave her a potion that put her to sleep once all four of the pale men were dead. After visiting with Marahay, I suggested that Caonabó send word to all the caciques of Quisqueya to gather in Xaraguá, which had still not been reached by the pale men, so that they might sit together and talk about this new menace in our region. We go tomorrow at dawn, by sea to Xaraguá. I will leave my Higuamota in the care of Simihena, who I know will keep her safe for me. I hope that we have seen the last of these men, but perhaps we have not.

A riddle too frightening to contemplate:

What if there are more of them? Many, many more of them?
Even more of them than there are of us,
just waiting to attack and destroy us for our gold?

Land at last! I rejoice to be back in my old home, back in Xaraguá. We immediately rushed to Behechio, who was extremely happy to see us alive. The other caciques had not yet arrived, so we told Behechio of our encounter with the pale men. He, too, had his own tales to share. From what he'd heard, there were indeed more of these men in Chief

Guacanagarí's region. Chief Guacanagarí was friendly with them, had even made a pact with them, offering them a settlement site in exchange for protection against the Kalinas. Consistent with what we had seen, the pale men in Marién also had a strong desire for gold. They asked for it constantly, as if it were food or drink, and were never satisfied with the amounts they were given. They had even frightened off some of the Kalinas.

"So these men are stronger than the Kalinas?" Caonabó asked.

Behechio said that from what he'd heard they were. He had not seen any himself, but had listened to accounts from those who had fled Marién and passed through his territory. There was one subchief from Marién who was now taking refuge in Baba and Bibi's house. Caonabó and I asked to see him, and Behechio sent for him immediately.

I did not wait for the subchief to come, but quickly went to Baba and Bibi's house, for I was most eager to see them. Like everyone else, Bibi seemed troubled. Only Baba was calm, saying if it took a menace to bring me back to Xaraguá, he was still delighted to see me again.

Eager to see the subchief from Marién, Caonabó soon arrived at Baba and Bibi's house, but the subchief was not there. According to Bibi, he had fled to the mountains to hide. Most of those who had seen the pale men did the same thing, Baba said, thinking they were visions of souls they had wronged in life who had returned to exact revenge on them.

Caonabó and I assured everyone that the pale men were not the Night Marchers we had heard about all our lives. They were people, he said. Like the Kalinas. They were cruel men who would not hesitate to harm an old woman or a child.

"I would like to see my nephew," I said, trying to calm things.

Bibi brought Guarocuyá out for me to see. How strong he looks. How handsome. The spitting image, I must admit, of his father. I wish there was more time to just sit and hold him, but we had very pressing matters at hand.

LAST QUARTER MOON, DAY 20

Caonabó's brother, Manicaotex, arrived at dusk with a large group of fighters. Being so much like his brother, both in appearance and in temperament, he instantly declared that we should take all our fighters to Marién to see for ourselves what the pale men were doing there.

There is no time to wait for the distant Chief Cotubanamá of Higüey. We will leave for Marién at dawn. Caonabó, Manicaotex, and I will go by sea with most of our fighters. Manicaotex's people will go by land. Behechio will remain in Xaraguá so we can have one cacique in place in one of our three regions. We no longer trust Chief Guacanagarí's loyalties. It is possible that he is no longer on our side. And if we have to fight him, for the sake of our land and our people, we will.

Our decision made, we lit no fires at dusk and sat inside Behechio's house all night. In case the pale men traveled at night, we did not want to make it easier for them to find us.

As I held my nephew Guarocuyá again, this time in the dark, I kept thinking of my Higuamota. What was she doing? Laughing? Crying? Was she thinking of me, just as I was thinking of her?

"Guarocuyá, tomorrow at dawn we leave to fight for you." I spoke these words in my nephew's ear the way I would like to have spoken them in Higuamota's. "We will all fight bravely for you and Higuamota and all of Quisqueya's children. If we do not finish the battle, it is your duty to finish it for us and it is your burden to succeed."

In the pitch-dark of the night, my brother's voice floated toward me from the opposite corner of the room.

"Anacaona," he said, "he is too young to understand."

Somehow I could feel it in a place so deep in me that it

has no top or bottom, no beginning or end. Perhaps Guarocuyá was too young to understand, but I know he heard me, because when I was done speaking, he softly squeezed my thumb before drifting off to sleep.

OUR SEASON OF WAR
First Quarter Moon, Day 1

Again, we are at sea. Caonabó, Manicaotex, and I are proudly dressed in our finest headdresses, strongest belts, and largest golden breastplates. Our warriors have their most agile, Kalina-style bows and arrows, which Caonabó had learned to make from Marahay's instructions. We also have the metal lightning rods from the dead pale men. We are more than prepared for war.

It was sad to leave Baba, Bibi, Behechio, and my nephew in Xaraguá. But I am comforted by the thought that I am on a journey that will protect all of Quisqueya's lands and her people. We are accompanied by at least twenty canoes full of skillful warriors, but there are moments when we lose sight of them when they fall in line behind us, obediently following the currents of the sea. Caonabó and Manicaotex are both quiet, resting for what's ahead. Their calm comforts me, though occasionally my thoughts float back to Maguana, to my Higuamota. I pray she is well. This is also my prayer for all our people.

First Quarter Moon, Day 3

How do I begin to describe what I have seen on Marién? We arrived on the shores at dusk. Since it was dark, we anchored our canoes and remained on the beach until dawn.

At dawn, we began to move inland but were quickly stopped by ten tall, moonfaced men armed with lightning rods. Again these men fired into the air, but as we had already spoken of these things to our fighters, only a few of them fled in fright, cowardly escaping to the sea, where many of them drowned as they attempted to reach their canoes.

Caonabó, Manicaotex, and I stepped forward to one who seemed to be the leader and offered him all the gold ornaments we were wearing. We even ordered our fighters to accept whatever they were given in exchange for their own ornaments, even their spears.

As this exchange was taking place, Caonabó pointed inland and spoke Chief Guacanagarí's name asking where he was. The leader started walking inland and motioned for us to follow him. As we trailed him, his men quickly gathered behind him, stepping between him and our fighters.

A large group of Chief Guacanagarí's people lined our path as we entered the village. They were all staring at us with a mixture of fear and hope, as though we were new heroic captives entering our captors' settlement.

We walked slowly to Chief Guacanagarí's house, moving through the enormous plaza out front, which was crowded with more of Guacanagarí's people. Many of them were roasting meat and preparing food in very large amounts, perhaps for both themselves and their visitors. On my left, I noticed some Marién men hanging from trees near the plaza walls, the bodies dangling above our heads. Caonabó and Manicaotex both stopped and looked up, horrified. I was especially shocked, for the way these men were apparently executed reminded me of the dream I had of being choked by the Kalina serpent god, Joulouca. I couldn't control the angry shiver running through my body. What could these men have done to deserve a death such as this? To be left in the sun where birds could peck at their open flesh?

Walking through the plaza, we saw more corpses on the ground. Some looked as though they'd recently had their hands cut off and were still bleeding as they lay unmoving in the soil. I was trembling with anger, but we had to take our time and inform ourselves further before we could do anything. Caonabó and Manicaotex quickly tried to shout some questions to Chief Guacanagarí's people, but they stared back blankly, looking absolutely dazed as though there was no explanation for what we were seeing.

Once we crossed the plaza, after that long walk filled with death, we reached Chief Guacanagarí's house. At his door lay a few of the pale men. Two of them were moaning, their bodies covered with large sores. One of Chief Guacanagarí's daughters, whom Behechio had once considered for a wife, was tending to the sick ones, giving them water and rubbing leaves over their sores. Most of the pale men looked similar to me, with the same light eyes and heavy body cover that reached from their shoulders down to their toes. But the ones with the sores were thinner and wore little covering and seemed truly distressed as they writhed in pain and screamed what sounded like prayers in their own language, to their own gods.

The leader motioned for us to stop at Chief Guacanagarí's doorstep. He exchanged some words with his men and pointed at us. It seemed as if they were asking each other whether they should allow us to enter Chief Guacanagarí's dwelling.

Impatient, Caonabó did not wait for them to come to a

decision. He called Chief Guacanagarí's name and respectfully requested for him to come out. Chief Guacanagarí
tottered out, wobbling on a wounded leg.

He had fallen, he explained, as though everything else
was normal. "And old bones do not heal too quickly."

"What is taking place here?" Caonabó asked. "Who are
these men?"

Chief Guacanagarí motioned to a large silk-cotton tree
at the side of his house. He signaled that we could sit on a
small mat under the tree and talk there. Chief Guacanagarí
looked over at the pale leader as though to ask permission
for this. The leader nodded. We followed Chief Guacanagarí
to the tree, with a group of the pale men trailing us.

Sitting under the tree, with the pale men standing over
us, Chief Guacanagarí quickly told the story of their
arrival, much as we had already heard it. These pale men
had arrived on three ships. One of the ships had been
destroyed by strong winds at sea. Chief Guacanagarí had
boarded their ship and welcomed their supreme leader
just as he would one of our caciques, offering him gifts of
parrots, cotton, and a gold belt. In exchange, their supreme
leader had offered him some new food and drink, which he
had shared with his men, and some beads and fruit-
scented water. Chief Guacanagarí had told the supreme
leader that he and his people were welcomed in Marién

and that he would do all he could to make them at ease. To prove this, Chief Guacanagarí had placed his hand on the supreme leader's ashy head of hair as a sign of honor and had ordered his people to build them a settlement, farther inland.

Soon after the supreme leader departed and left these men here in Marién, the men began beating and killing the people of Marién, forcing the women — including his own daughters — to disappear with them at night. Through hand signals, they continually expressed their desire for gold, forcing his people to dig in the mountains and mine the rivers from dusk to dawn.

When one of the pale men heard Chief Guacanagarí say *tuob*, the Marién word for gold, he disrespectfully poked his lightning rod at Chief Guacanagarí's head, thinking, it seemed, that Chief Guacanagarí was discussing with us ways of finding more gold for him and his men.

Chief Guacanagarí looked up at the pale man and nodded and Caonabó and I did the same so that we would be allowed a few more moments to speak in peace.

"I believe their leader might have been in my region looking for gold." Caonabó was purposely trying to use the word gold, and each time he did we looked up at the pale men and they shook their heads and smiled as though their treasures were mounting every time we uttered it.

"What did you do to him?" Chief Guacanagarí asked.

"We sent him back where he came from," Caonabó answered cautiously, for we were still not certain where Chief Guacanagarí's loyalties truly lay.

Chief Guacanagarí appeared saddened by this. He covered his face with his hands and moaned for some time.

"What shall we do now?" Chief Guacanagarí asked in desperation. "They are strong and have weapons we do not have. They have already killed many of our people who have tried to fight them. They will not even let us bury them. They want the corpses out in the open as a sign to others. The only thing that can save us is that they seem to not yet understand what we say, except for the word for gold, *tuob*, which they have already learned."

The leader poked his lightning rod at Chief Guacanagarí's head once more and repeated "*tuob*."

We all nodded and uttered, "*Tuob, tuob*," even adding "we will find *tuob*."

"We will appease them until dark," Caonabó said, "then my people will fight them."

Chief Guacanagarí looked frightened, as if fearing the punishment that might follow such an action. He seemed unsure still whether these were men or gods, but whatever they were he feared them.

"Your people need not take part," Manicaotex told

Chief Guacanagarí. "If there is retribution, you could also say that Caonabó and Manicaotex battled and defeated them."

I was glad to see Manicaotex so certain of our victory, but could we really defeat these men? We certainly had more fighters than they did. Many were due to arrive from inland at dusk. And if some of the Marién people joined with us, then we would have even more.

Chief Guacanagarí appeared not only troubled but tired. Whatever had become of the jovial man who had visited us in Maguana? The one who had held my daughter in his arms and envisioned that one day she might marry one of his sons? I could no longer see any trace of that man. The pale phantoms had taken him away.

Chief Guacanagarí buried his face in his hands once more. Realizing that he would be of no use to us, Caonabó turned his attention back to the pale men. He got up to face them and pointed to a distant mountain while saying once more the word *tuob*. Finally the pale men became aware that he was suggesting that there was gold in those mountains and we would get it for them.

Seeing a battle plan taking shape in Caonabó's mind, I whispered to Chief Guacanagarí, "Do not fear. We will put our men to work for them for the day. But tonight as they sleep . . ."

Chief Guacanagarí motioned that he did not want to hear any more. We had neither his blessing nor his disapproval.

"We must do this," I whispered to him, "so that Quisqueya can live, so my Higuamota can marry one of your young sons."

And having nearly as many wives as Behechio, he had many young sons from which my Higuamota could choose.

Leaving Chief Guacanagarí behind, Caonabó signaled for the pale men to follow us up a trail to the mountains. The pale men motioned for a large group of Marién people to follow us as well. Caonabó kept saying the word *tuob* to the pale men. And as we marched up a trail toward the mountains, I felt as though I was suddenly journeying to an uncertain place. All around us, burial plots had been dug up, bones thrown aside, and golden objects removed from sacred soil. Nearby, a pregnant woman lay dead, her still bulging belly leaning slightly away from her body. Corpses were strewn all along our path, heads separated from bodies. The body of one dead child was leaning against a post, as if he had been carefully hooked there.

Each step was agonizing as we walked past the high wooden dwelling built from the salvaged pieces of the pale men's wrecked ship. It was almost as large as one of our plazas, but more narrow. Knowing that Marién people were probably forced to build it pained me even more.

As we walked past the dwelling, the pale men called for others inside to join them. We were now a large group, heading for the mountains, looking for the gold that might soothe them, until dark.

LATER

We spent the day bent over in the scalding sun, panning and mining for gold. It was difficult work and many of our people fell into the river, too weary to continue. They were quickly replaced by some Mariéns whom the pale men called forward. Manicaotex knew where gold could be found and he led the pale men to it. Our fighters worked arduously, turning over rocks in rivers and digging craters in the sides of the mountains to find a pile as tall and as wide as one of these men.

As they worked in the hot sun looking for gold, I wondered if our people were not tiring themselves too much. Would we be able to fight later?

As the sun set and it became too dark to look for gold, our fighters were at last permitted to gather some food to eat. Rather than food, Caonabó and Manicaotex and I commanded them to collect hot peppers, which we would use in our attacks on the settlement.

By the time the moon surfaced, we had also collected rocks and pieces of dry wood with which to begin a fire. The pale men were lazy, and once the Marién workers had moved all the gold we had collected to their dwelling, they gathered there, drinking the corn wine and the food the Marién women brought them. Soon the torches faded and they fell asleep.

We waited for the torches in Chief Guacanagarí's house to fade, too. We had not returned to see him, for we did not want to endanger whatever promises he had made to the pale men's supreme leader concerning their protection. Still, after dark, even though Manicaotex's land warriors had not yet arrived, many of Chief Guacanagarí's men surfaced in the plaza, with spears and sharpened stones for our attack.

We had to move quickly, ordering a charge toward the pale men's settlement. The true gods of our ancestors were certainly with us, for we all acted swiftly and as though we were one being, different limbs of one body.

Some of our men wrapped hot peppers in dried banana leaves, set them aflame, and threw them into the pale men's quarters. In spite of the peppered smoke, many of our men also leaped inside and bravely battled against the lightning rods with stones and spears. I could not see Caonabó for some time, but watched as many of the pale men stepped out in the moonlight with bloody heads, leaned forward, and fell to the ground. Woefully, many Marién women, who were in the dwelling, lost their lives as well. I saw Manicaotex carry several of them out, only to lay them on the ground to die. Many of our men were lost, too, with large holes dug into their bodies by the lightning rods or deep wounds carved by sharp, long knives. I had my chance to wrap my fingers around the neck of one young invader as he stumbled toward one of the dying women I was cradling in my arms, but my heart softened and I kept to my task, which at that moment was to help this woman die.

Soon, the pale men's entire settlement was ablaze, and in the glare of that light I saw Caonabó and Manicaotex running to me.

I lowered the girl onto the grass and grabbed Caonabó's hand and held it as strongly as I could. The flames were now leaping up to the sky. Many of Chief Guacanagarí's men looked stunned, but satisfied. There were only two pale men left, the sickly ones at Chief Guacanagarí's door-step, who were near death, anyway.

"We must go now," Caonabó shouted to Manicaotex and our fighters. We started running for the beach, where we had anchored our canoes. Our men hastily followed us, their footsteps as loud as thunder. Reaching the beach, we quickly climbed into our canoes. Our retreat was swift, and soon Marién was behind us.

First Quarter Moon, Day 4

Caonabó, Manicaotex, and I did not speak very much on the journey back to Maguana. We were all too startled by what we had seen and done. It was only when the sun came up that I noticed a large cut on Caonabó's arm. One of the pale men had sliced him with a knife. We were without a healer, so Manicaotex had to treat him. All we had in abundance was seawater, which our all fighters used to treat their wounds.

Half Moon, Day 5

We approached Maguana with some trepidation. Would more pale men be there? Were our people their prisoners?

From the beach, all seemed calm. But the calm of the seas and the stillness of the wind could be deceiving.

We marched toward our home with our fighters closely behind us, ready to fight again if we had to. But thankfully, we did not have to fight. Maguana was as it has always been, green and lush and tranquil.

Higuamota was brought to us soon after we arrived. I ran to her and scooped her up in my arms, watching her awaken with a smile. Caonabó and I took turns embracing her and thanking Simihena for looking after her. Manicaotex will be staying with us until those of his fighters who went to Marién by land return.

HALF MOON, DAY 7

Even as we wait with Manicaotex to hear from his fighters, we sent word to Behechio of our victory in Marién. What great joy it gives me to hold Higuamota in my arms again, to sit with Caonabó and Manicaotex and share a tranquil meal, to carve a symbol with Simihena to place in the temple to thank our ancestors for watching over us, to see Marahay cooking her pepper pot again. Only now can I think of how closely we had all come to losing our lives.

Full Moon, Day 13

No word yet from Behechio or from Manicaotex's fighters. Did they face more danger? Have they been defeated? And what of Xaraguá?

Full Moon, Day 15

No word also from Chief Guacanagarí. I thought he would have sent a messenger to reproach or praise us. I pray that if there are remaining able-bodied pale men in Marién, they will not exact revenge on him for our actions, for it is all too clear that these invaders were no different than the Kalinas, who would destroy us all, if they could. Maybe we will encounter these pale creatures again, but we will continue to combat them, just as we are slowly learning to combat the Kalinas. For we have no choice. Our people's survival depends on it.

Last Quarter Moon, Day 19

We have word from Manicaotex's men. They returned by land, stopping in Maguá, Higüey, Xaraguá then Maguana to be certain that there were no pale men left in our regions. (The two sick ones that Chief Guacanagarí's daughter was looking after died of the mysterious illness that had covered their bodies in sores.) Behechio and Chief Cotubanamá of Higüey sent us cages of beautiful birds — eagles, falcons, hawks, geese, and doves — to honor our victory. We are triumphant! At least for now.

Before Manicaotex left us to return to Maguana, we had a feast to thank the gods for our victory. Caonabó and Manicaotex played mock battles along with our fighters. We had ball games both in daylight and at night. We danced, sang ballads, and recited several tales. However, the longest tale of all was mine. It was an account of our season of war. This tale was long not because I described every detail of the battle but because I also spoke of the days that came before it.

Sitting in the plaza, with Caonabó at my side and Higuamota in my arms, I told of the day of my marriage to Caonabó, of my arrival in Maguana, and of the birth of my daughter. I also told of the Night Marchers and the frog children and of Mácocael and our ancestors from the caves. I told such a lengthy tale because I did not want our battle with the pale men to become the only story our people would ever recite from now on. For we had other stories, too, happy as well as sad ones. Our encounter with the pale men was only a small piece of that story. Surely an important piece, but not the most important.

Yes, I want our victory over the pale men to be a tale

that will inspire us when we have other battles to fight, one that reminds us that, like the Kalinas, we are a strong and powerful people. I do want it to be a story whose veracity the young ones will ask me to confirm when I am an old woman, a story that my Higuamota will tell and retell to her own children. But I do not want it to become the only story we ever have to share with one another. It cannot be. It must not be.

Epilogue

Unfortunately, this was not the last that Anacaona saw of the Spanish invaders. A few months later, in November 1493, their supreme leader, Christopher Columbus, returned from Spain with seventeen ships, 1700 men, ammunition, hunting dogs, and horses. In revenge for the attack on Columbus's settlement in Chief Guacanagarí's territory — a settlement the Spaniards had named La Navidad (The Nativity), since it was established on Christmas Day — Chief Caonabó was captured by Columbus's men. Caonabó's brother Manicaotex brought together thousands of fighters from all over the island in an effort to rescue him, but Manicaotex and his warriors were overcome by the Spanish. Defeated, Manicaotex was also captured and placed on board the same ship as his brother, a ship that was to bring them to Europe, where their fate would be decided by the king and queen of Spain. The ship capsized at sea, during what is believed to have been Caonabó and Manicaotex's last valiant battle. Everyone on board, including the brothers, perished.

After her husband's death, a sad yet resolute Anacaona returned with her daughter to Xaraguá to rule with her brother Behechio. When Behechio died, she became the sole ruler of Xaraguá, one of the last remaining and most powerful Taíno leaders on the island. However, the fact that the Spaniards had managed to capture two of the island's most capable warriors intimidated the other caciques and cacicas, including Anacaona, into following Columbus's brutal new order, which demanded a quarterly tariff of a "large bell" full of gold and twenty-five pounds of cotton from every Taíno over fourteen years old. To make sure that this tariff was paid, Columbus established a system of forced labor in which Taínos were made to work on cotton and tobacco plantations and in gold mines. Overworked and malnourished, and often flogged and tortured, the Taínos succumbed to starvation as well as such European diseases as smallpox, malaria, yellow fever, influenza, and measles. Others burned down their villages, fled to the mountains, or killed themselves.

To quell the last remaining sparks of resistance, Columbus's men carried out regular raids, capturing and killing hundreds of Taíno fighters. In 1503, the new Spanish governor, Nicholas Ovando, requested a meeting with Anacaona. At the feast, to which the beautiful Anacaona is reported to have arrived covered only in flowers, Ovando ordered his men to kill the more than eighty Taínos she had assembled to greet him. These Taínos were either shot, clubbed to death, or set on fire. Because of her high standing, Anacaona was spared a fiery or bloody end. Instead she was hanged at twenty-nine years old.

Anacaona's death was the final blow to the upper echelon of Taíno society. Anacaona's nephew, Guarocuyá, also known as Cacique Henri, survived and retreated to the mountains, where he would continue to fight the Spanish decades after her death. It is not known what became of Anacaona's daughter.

LIFE IN HAITI
IN 1490

HISTORICAL NOTE

In the Taíno language, the word Taíno means "noble and good," which is exactly how the Taínos were regarded, by themselves and others. It is estimated that there were 200,000 Taínos on Quisqueya — the island is now more commonly called Hispaniola — before Columbus arrived in 1492. Fifty years later, there were only a few hundred.

Before they were abruptly "discovered" by Columbus, the Taínos lived quietly in a primarily agricultural society. Their land was extremely fertile, covered with flowing rivers and lush, bountiful fruit trees. Their skies were full of birds, among them eagles, hawks, and geese. At night they trembled at the sounds of bats and owls fluttering about, for they considered them bad omens.

There were several societal groups to which a Taíno could belong, among them the *naborías*, or servant class; the nitaínos, subchiefs or regional leaders and, at the very top, the caciques, or supreme rulers. Because Taíno society was matriarchal, one could only inherit a ruling position through a female relative, the way Anacaona's uncle, for example, inherited his rule from her grandmother.

For food, the Taínos farmed their mounds of land, or *conucos*, where they grew such staples as yucca, maize (corn), sweet potatoes, beans, squash, peanuts, and chili peppers. For their hammocks and their very sparse body coverings, they grew cotton, which they then spun into cloth. They also cultivated tobacco, which was widely used. For meat, they hunted birds, iguanas, snakes, and hutias, a species of small rodent. At sea, they caught fish, manatees, turtles, crabs, oysters, lobsters, and conch. The canoes they used for fishing as well as travel were carved from large tree trunks and were able to carry as many as fifty to a hundred of them. They also used hollowed tree trunks to make their drums, which were among the many musical instruments they possessed. For their large feasts and celebrations, called *areitos*, they also crafted maracas or gourd rattles. During their celebrations, they would tell stories, sing ballads, perform dances, take part in mock battles, and play a very popular, volleyball-like game called a batey. While playing the ball game, they would wear round protective disks or elbow stones. The elbow stones were among the many beautiful objects they created. Others included mortars and pestles, ceramics, elaborate necklaces, breastplates, and ear and nose rings made from shells, bone beads, and semiprecious stones. The most refined carvers among them — Anacaona was reportedly one of those — crafted ceremonial chairs called *duhos* as well as religious sculptures and amulets called *zemis*.

Before Christopher Columbus arrived on the island in 1492, the biggest threat to the Taínos was the island Caribs, or Kalinas, who often raided their villages, killing their men and carrying away their women as part of a practice of bride capture. Though the Caribs were by far the better warriors, the Taínos nevertheless had certain weapons with which to defend themselves. They had spears, bows and poisoned arrows, clubs, and sharpened rocks called *cibas*. Though most of the Taínos of Hispaniola (now comprised of Haiti and the Dominican Republic) vanished in the Americas' first genocide, there are many traces left of them today. Remnants of Taíno life include hammocks, barbecue, and tobacco. Among the Taíno words that have made their way into our vocabulary are hurricane, canoe, tuna, and iguana. It is believed that most if not all of Hispaniola's Taínos were exterminated, but there are groups of people in the Dominican Republic, Puerto Rico, and Cuba who identify themselves as Taíno. Some have even proven themselves to be legitimate descendants of the Taínos through DNA tests. Before

1492, the island which would later be called Española (little Spain) and Hispaniola, by the Spanish, was interchangeably called Quisqueya, Bohio, and Ayiti by the Taínos. We set this story in Haiti because Xaraguá, the region Anacaona ruled, is believed to have been part of what is now modern Haiti.

ANACAONA'S GRANDMOTHER
(Name unknown, Cacica of Xaraguá)

GUAMAYTO = ANACAONA'S UNCLE
(Name unknown, Cacique of Xaraguá)

BIBI = BABA
(Name unknown, Anacaona's mother)   (Name unknown, Anacaona's father)

MANICOATEX — CAONABÓ = ANACAONA — BEHECHIO = YANUBA (First wife) / THIRTY WIVES (Names unknown)

HIGUAMOTA

GUAROCUYÁ

Ruler

ANACAONA'S FAMILY TREE

ANACAONA, niece of the cacique of Xaraguá, was raised to rule her province. She married Chief Caonabó of Maguana, and left her people to live in her husband's land. She was captured by the Spanish in 1493, and hanged.

BEHECHIO, brother of Anacaona, became the cacique of Xaraguá in the early 1490s. He is reported to have had more than thirty wives.

CAONABÓ, husband of Anacaona, was cacique of the province of Maguana. He was captured by the Spanish in 1493, and perished in a Spanish prison ship.

MANICAOTEX, brother of Caonabó, brought thousands of fighters to rescue Caonabó, but he was defeated. He died with his brother.

GUAROCUYÁ, also known as Cacique Henri, was the son of Behechio and the nephew of Anacaona. Raised by Franciscan priests, he battled the Spaniards for more than a decade, long after his aunt and father died.

HIGUAMOTA was the daughter of Anacaona and Caonabó.

OTHER NOTABLE TAÍNO LEADERS

COTUBANAMÁ, cacique of Higüey, a southern region of the island. He fought the Spanish colonists for many years to maintain his region's sovereignty. He was eventually captured and hanged.

GUACANAGARÍ, cacique of Marién, a northern region of the island. He was one of the first to welcome Columbus to Hispaniola. Seeking protection against the Kalinas, who often invaded this area, he offered Columbus a place to build a settlement and became an adviser to the Spanish invaders.

GUARIONEX, cacique of Maguá. His name means Lord of Many People. He died at sea along with Chief Caonabó.

HIGUANAMA, cacica of Higüey before Cotubanamá. She was captured by the Spanish and is believed to have perished at sea with Guarionex and Caonabó.

MAYOBANEX, a regional chief in the Maguá region. He hid Guarionex from the Spanish until they were both eventually captured.

Portrait of Queen Anacaona painted by a contemporary artist.

Behechio, Anacaona's brother and cacique of Xaraguá, painted by a contemporary artist.

Anacaona with her maidens.

A ceremonial throne, used by the Taínos, decorated with special carvings.

Woodcuts by an Italian man, Girolamo Benzoni, who visited Haiti in the mid-1500s, show the bananas and other fruit trees of Haiti (top), and the unique sailing vessels used by the native fishermen (bottom).

The Spanish explorer Alonso de Ojeda meets with a cacique of the West Indies.

Alonso de Ojeda and his men battle the natives during their expedition to the West Indies. The Spanish conquered and destroyed large percentages of the populations they encountered in the West Indian islands.

Chief Caonabó is captured by the Spanish in 1493.

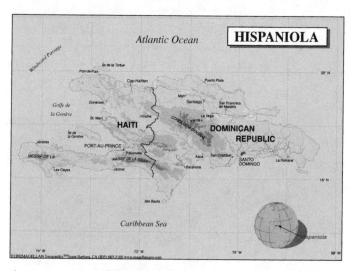

A contemporary map of Haiti. Xaraguá was located in the southwestern part of modern-day Haiti.

A Sample of Taíno Words

Ana: flower

areito: a Taíno ceremony that includes narrative poems, ballads, music, dances, ball games, and mock battles

Atabey: goddess of freshwater fertility (Yúcahu's mother)

ayiti: mountainous land, slippery land

Baba: father

bagua: sea

barbacoa: a stand for roasting meat; the original source of the current-day "barbecue"

batey: ceremonial ball court or plaza, also the name used for the Taíno ball game similar to today's volleyball

Bibi: mother; the word *toa* is also used for "mother."

bohío: a common Taíno residence

cacica: female supreme chief, or ruler

cacique: male supreme chief, or ruler

caney: the house of the chief or ruler; longhouse

canoa: canoe or boat

caona: yellow gold. Another word for gold is *tuob*.

casabi: cassava made from the yucca plant, a staple of the Taíno diet

cayo: island

ciba: a sharpened stone used as a tool or weapon

coa: a wooden stick used in conuco-style farming and also as a weapon in mock battles

cokí: frog

colibri: hummingbird

conuco: Taíno farming land; also refers to the Taíno method of farming

digo: plant used to wash the body

duho: a ceremonial chair or stool used by Taíno leaders

iguana: a large lizard

jamaca (hamaia): hammock

jurakan: storm, hurricane

Kalina: Island Carib; an enemy people

manicato: "strong," a courageous person

maraca: a gourd rattle; still used today in Caribbean music

Matunherí: Your Highness, Most Highest One

mayohaboa: a Taíno drum that the Taínos referred to as "the voice of the gods"

naboría: Taíno servant class

nagua: women's skirt

nigua: a flealike insect that penetrates the skin to lay its eggs, causing itching and ulcers

nitaíno: Taíno "noble"

opia: spirit of ancestors or the dead

siani: married woman

tabacú: tobacco

tuna: something from the water

turey: sky

uicu: a fermented drink made from the juice of the yucca

yaque: river

yaya: spirit of the tree, supreme ancestor

zemi: a sculpture created for religious use; often made out of wood or stone

ABOUT THE AUTHOR

Edwidge Danticat was born in Port-au-Prince, Haiti, and is the author of two adult novels, *Breath, Eyes, Memory* and *The Farming of Bones*, and two collections of short stories, *Krik? Krak!* and *The Dew Breaker*. She has also written a young adult novel, *Behind the Mountains*, which appears in Orchard Books' First Person Fiction series.

Ms. Danticat has always wanted to write about Anacaona, ever since she heard about her as a little girl.

"I was immediately fascinated by Anacaona," she says, "because here was a woman who was not only a warrior, poet, and storyteller but also one of our first diplomats."

Re-creating a diary for Anacaona was a challenge she was happy to take on, but a challenge nonetheless. First of all, the Taínos, by most accounts, did not read or write. So how, then, to create a diary, even a fictional one, for someone who did not write as we know it today?

"Even though the Taínos had no written language," she explains, "they had images and symbols through which they told their stories. I see this diary as a series of images and symbols that could have been put away by a storyteller like Anacaona to be interpreted later. Taíno artifacts are being discovered all the time. With each piece found, the story of the Taíno people gets more and more specific, more and more defined."

Although she did as much research as possible to recreate young Anacaona's life, Ms. Danticat created many fictional characters, including Cuybio, Bayaci, Marahay, and Yeybona.

"There were probably lots of people like this in Anacaona's life," she says, "even though we don't know their names." The names she missed knowing most are those of Anacaona's parents. "In terms of what we know of Taíno history, we mostly have accounts and names recorded for people who were around during the Taínos' 'encounter' with Christopher Columbus and his men, but at least many Taíno words have made their way down to us, including Baba and Bibi (Mother and Father)."

Ms. Danticat was most thrilled to write this fictional diary of Anacaona for another very special reason.

"My mother was born in Léogâne," she says, referring

to a Haitian town that is generally thought to have been at the center of Xaraguá, where Anacaona ruled. "Thus in some very primal way, Anacaona has always been in my blood and I remain, in the deepest part of my soul, one of her most faithful subjects."

For Rose, Denise, and Zora Danticat
I love you, Daddy.

ACKNOWLEDGMENTS

Grateful acknowledgment is made for permission to reprint the following:

Cover painting by Tim O'Brien

Page 170 (top): Portrait of Queen Anacaona painted by a contemporary artist, Ulrick Jean-Pierre, New Orleans, Louisiana.

Page 170 (bottom): Behechio, Anacaona's brother and cacique of Xaraguá, painted by a contemporary artist, Ulrick Jean-Pierre, New Orleans, Louisiana.

Page 171 (top): Anacaona with her maidens, North Wind Picture Archives, Alfred, Maine.

Page 171 (bottom): A ceremonial throne, Musee de l'Homme, Paris, France/ www.bridgeman.co.uk.

Page 172 (top): Fruit trees of Haiti, Woodcut by Girolamo Benzoni, North Wind Picture Archives, Alfred, Maine.

Page 172 (bottom): Haitian fishing vessels, Woodcut by Girolamo Benzoni, The Granger Collection, New York, New York.

OTHER BOOKS IN THE ROYAL DIARIES SERIES

ELIZABETH I
Red Rose of the House of Tudor
by Kathryn Lasky

CLEOPATRA VII
Daughter of the Nile
by Kristiana Gregory

MARIE ANTOINETTE
Princess of Versailles
by Kathryn Lasky

ISABEL
Jewel of Castilla
by Carolyn Meyer

ANASTASIA
The Last Grand Duchess
by Carolyn Meyer

NZINGHA
Warrior Queen of Matamba
by Patricia C. McKissack

KAIULANI
The People's Princess
by Ellen Emerson White

Library of Congress Cataloging-in-Publication Data

Danticat, Edwidge, 1969-
Anacaona, Golden Flower / by Edwidge Danticat. — 1st ed.
p. cm. — (The royal diaries)
Summary: Beginning in 1490, Anacaona keeps a record of her life
as a possible successor to the supreme chief of Xaragua, as wife of the chief
of Maguana, and as a warrior battling the first white men to arrive
in the West Indies, ravenous for gold.
ISBN 0-439-49906-2
1. Anacaona, d. 1504 — Juvenile fiction. [1. Anacaona, d. 1504 — Fiction.
2. Taino Indians — Fiction.   3. Indians of the West Indies — Fiction.
4. Kings, queens, rulers, etc. — Fiction.   5. Haiti — History — To 1791 —
Fiction.   6. America — Discovery and exploration — Spanish — Fiction.
7. Diaries — Fiction.]   I. Title.   II. Series.
PZ7.D2385An 2005
[Fic] — dc22   2004012560

10   9   8   7   6   5   4   3   2   1   05   06   07   08   09

The display type was set in Galahad.
The text type was set in Augereau.
Book design by Elizabeth B. Parisi
Photo research by Amla Sanghvi

Printed in the U.S.A. 23
First edition, April 2005